never enough

NEVER ENOUGH
by Byron Woolfe

Published by Pulp Culture Press

44 Race Street
San Jose, CA 95126

www.pulpculturepress.com

ISBN: 978-1-59362-326-5

POD Edition

"I'll bet you're harmless! I've heard about you automobile salesmen. And I never heard of one being called harmless."

"You've been listening to the wrong people," Harry said.

EDITORS NOTES

Harry Baker was a sailor, and like most sailors, I suppose Haryy could never get enough. He has, as the cover copy suggested, an "Insatiate desire…" which sounds really ominous and kind of dangerous but in the end, just means he is super-horny all the time. But Harry, despite all that, is a decent guy; all he needs is to settle down with a girl who wants it just as much as he does.

That pretty much sums up **Never Enough** by Byron Woolfe, which was published in 1958 by Saber Books and distributed by Western News Company. This book is goofy by our standards today, but it was not only scandalous in 1958 it was actually entered into evidence in a 1960 court trial of Western News Company, which was indicted by a grand jury no less, in a case where the company was accused and found guilty of using the US Mail to distribute obscene material.

Now while I would not give this book to a child to read, there is nothing in the book that is by our standards today, obscene. And yet here it was being held up as one of several examples of books that were obscene enough that the mail should not have been used to distribute them.
The trial took two months, and the jury found the company guilty on six counts of using a common carrier "for carriage in interstate commerce of certain obscene, lewd, lascivious, and filthy books, from Fresno, California, to City News Agency in the City of Kalamazoo, in Kalamazoo County," *United States v. West Coast News Company*, 228 F. Supp. 171, 174 n.4 (W.D. Mich. 1964).

The jury was thankfully spared the agony of having each of the books read aloud in their entirety in court. However, a great deal of time was spent on the issue of how to present the books in evidence to the jurors. There is a concept cited in the case summary that says that something needs to be considered as a whole and not just in an excerpt. Many pre-trial motions were spent on how to consider the books, which the prosecutors went to great lengths to say were not themselves on trial.

Summaries were indeed written for each of the books, though, and the one for Never Enough seemed to sum up the book pretty well;

The main character begins his story by leaving the navy in Norfolk, meeting a prostitute in a bar, having sexual intercourse with her, and being rolled. In a quite unrelated fashion, he then becomes a used car salesman, and we learn that no woman has ever satisfied him.
The story is then a series of episodes between the main character and willing women. After much intercourse, unsuccessful seduction, bizarre

flashbacks, and a nymphomaniac from nowhere, the sexual craving of our character finally leads him to a young girl with whom he is satisfied.

The sexual equipment of the characters is grossly emphasized. The sex acts all culminate in wild pleasure. Sadism and masochism are featured. Characters leave and enter the story with no apparent relationship with the story. 142 pages.

And that sums it up for the book, for Harry, and for everyone in the story, although I will say this: There is a short passage of the book where one of the characters recounts some time aboard a naval vessel in wartime. I kind of felt that was real and probably could have been expanded a bit. While Byron Woolfe was most likely a pseudonym, he is credited for several books from this time, all published by Saber Books. Western News was found guilty on six of the 19 counts brought against them, which more than likely put them out of business. The publisher of the books themselves actually printed pleas for help from their readers, asking them to write letters of support to their attorneys and pointing out that the government's uptight attitude towards the depiction of sex had "MOST THINKING PEOPLE AGREE THAT THIS OSTRICH-LIKE APPROACH TO SEX IS QUITE WRONG AND HAS CAUSED GREAT HARM TO THE MENTAL HEALTH OF VAST NUMBERS OF PEOPLE" (the all caps is theirs). They also pointed out that the literary value of their books was not the point, it was the readers ability to choose which was at stake.

While the publisher's opinion might be so much hyperbole it is interesting and actually alarming to see how much was spent and how much time wasted over what is in our regards now a pretty innocuous book. People no doubt lost their livelihoods over this issue, and as we seem to be turning back the clock on so many things in our society, it's worth looking at this book and it's place in history as a sort of cautionary tale.

As with our other **Pulp Culture Press** reprints, we have added clipart and AI-generated art (and to be honest, I can't say that the clipart we bought to go with this was not generated by AI. This was done to make this edition a little more of a nice thing for your bookshelf. The original cover is now on the back and a new cover that is a little more attractive graces the front of this reprint.

If you would like to read more about the Western News Company trial, you can scan the QR code below for a rundown on a site called Casetext.

CHAPTER ONE

Shorty, the cab driver, was suffering. He was sitting alone in his hack on East Main Street about a block from the burlesque house. Business had been lousy all morning. A few sailors were ambling along the street but none of them seemed to want to go anywhere.

Every time Shorty had to sit for long spells in his cab with nothing to do, he got to thinking about Frances who was without a doubt the prettiest whore in Norfolk, and Shorty was crazy as hell about her.

The more he had to sit the more he thought about her. He wished to hell he had a pocket full of dough. He'd go up to her place right now. Shorty reached into his pocket and pulled out what money he had. There were only four lousy dollars, and sixty percent of that belonged to Hank, the owner of the cab. Shorty snorted. He couldn't go to see Frances with this chicken feed. She wouldn't even give him a feel for four lousy bucks. And anyway, if he spent the four bucks, Hank might come along and check up on him. Hank could get awful nasty if you tried to pull some thing over on him, like saying you hadn't taken in a dime when actually you had taken in four bucks. You couldn't fool Hank. He'd been in the cab busines too long. Hank could look at a guy and tell if he was lying or not, and he was liable to have a couple of his pals rough you up a bit. It didn't pay to play anyway but straight with Hank.

Shorty kept right on sitting there and thinking about Frances and getting more upset all the time. He was even beginning to breathe harder, just from picturing her in his mind. Yep, he sure wished he had himself some money. Some real dough. Lots of dough. Boy,
that would be the deal! If he had that kind of money he'd set Frances up irl a swell apartment. He'd buy her a Cadillac. He pictured himself tossing ·a few grand in her lap and saying, "Here, Frances, go some where and buy yourself one of them mink coats, and some glad rags to go with it."

Yessir, if he had plenty of dough he'd keep Frances all to himself. No more goddamn sailors for her. He'd tell her, "Now listen here, Frances, I don't want you messing around no damn more. If you're going to spend my dough you gotta be strictly my babe. Nobody else's, see? And I don't wanta catch none of them goddamn sailors 'round here neither!"

Four lousy dollars. What a crime! He wondered what kind of mood Frances was in this morning. Maybe she'd be interested in the four bucks, who knows? Shorty licked his lips. He'd be taking a chance of Hank getting sore as hell, but maybe he'd get lucky and make up the money before Hank found out. Shorty jammed on the starter and swung the cab away from the curb. He had to see Frances; he had to have himself some loving; that's all there was to it. When Frances opened the door to her apartment to see who had knocked, Shorty scooted in like he was afraid she might slam the door in his face.

"'Mornin', Frances, how you feeling this morning?"

Frances turned and surveyed the little man coolly, and with suspicion. "Why?" Frances was a beautiful girl, there was no denying it. She was wearing a light blue terry cloth bathrobe, fastened tightly about her mid–section, and the color of it went wonderfully well with her blond hair and blue eyes and white skin.

"I had to see you this morning, Frances, I just had to. I think about you all the time, you know that. I been sitting in my cab all morning, just dreaming my head off about you, honey. I 'just had to see you."

"Why?"

"Aw, cut it out, Frances honey. I got to have some loving. I got to love you a little, honey,"

"You got twenty bucks?"

Shorty pulled out the four dollars, "I only got four lousy bucks, honey. Business is terrible. How about it? Just one time for four bucks."

"Don't make me laugh," she said. "Four bucks? I wouldn't let you kiss my little finger for four bucks. You know my price. Twenty bucks or get out."

Shorty was sweating, Now that he'd seen her he wanted her ten times as bad as before,
"It's all the money I got, Frances honey. Honest it's every penny I got. Here, you can search my pockets, Listen, I know you're worth twenty. Hell, I'd give you a hundred if I had it, but I ain't. Come on, sugar, be a good scout. Tell you what, I'll bring you sixteen more later. You know you can trust me, so how about it, huh? Here, take the four dollars."

"You're breaking my heart," sneered Frances. "Why don't you run down to see Helen? She'll fix you up good for four dollars. She's more your speed any way."

"Helen's a dog," Shorty complained. "I wouldn't give her two bits. She's like the Grand Canyon. Ain't got no personality, neither, Chews gum all the time. Anything I can't stand is a woman chewing gum in my ear whilst I'm loving her. Runs me batty."

"Tough," said Frances,· "Well, you might as well run along, little man. If you manage to dig up twenty bucks somewhere, come back. Otherwise don't bother me."

"I said I'd pay you soon's I get it. Don't, you trust me? You know me? Shorty? We been friends a long time, honey. I steered many a guy to you."

"You got your cut."

"You mean you won't trust old Shorty?"

"I'm not running an installment business, little man. Now go get yourself some money or don't come hack." Frances sat on the sofa and let the bathrobe fall from her lovely legs. Shorty stared and nearly flipped his lid. He just had to have some of that, he just had to!

He jerked off his wristwatch. "Tell you what, honey, you can hold my watch for security. It's a swell watch, cost a lot of money. You hold this watch 'til I bring the other sixteen bucks. how about that?"

"Nothing doing. You probably lifted that piece of junk off a sailor, any-way. All I'm interested in, little man, is dollars. The green stuff."

Shorty pleaded some more, but he could see he was getting nowhere with the beautiful Frances. When it came to demanding her price her heart was as cold as a bucket of ice. He guessed he didn't really blame her though. She was certainly worth every penny of twenty bucks. He reckoned he'd been with just about every whore in Norfolk, and not a one of 'em could make it half as interesting as Frances. But she was all busi-ness before you paid her and she let her hair down. Somehow her cold, calculating way had a strange appeal to him, made him want her all the more. He couldn't understand it. All he knew was that every time he got hold of a twenty he couldn't wait to come and make love to Frances.

"Damn," he moaned now miserably, "I wish to hell I knew where I could lay my hands on some dough!"

Frances smiled for the first time, and studied the little runt through her long lashes. She knew he was wild about her. She even liked him in a small way. She even thought of giving him a little, but that would never do. Once a girl in her business started giving it away for free, it soon became a habit. None of that for her! She had what the guys wanted, and she made them pay the price. Every last one of them. The one thing in this world Frances craved was money. Money meant security. Nothing else did. She saved it and hoarded it like a regular miser. She had sense enough to know that her beauty was her fortune, hut that someday her beauty would fade, and that now she'd better make hay while the sun was shining.

"I know how you can make some money," she said. Shorty was all ears. "How?"

"Haven't you heard? The Fleet is due in today. There'll he thousands of sailors hitting Norfolk with money in their jeans and their tongues hanging out. Ought to he easy to roll a couple of them."

Shorty brightened. "Say, I forgot about that! Sure, the Fleet's coming in, that's right. I'll get on down to the base in my cab and see if I can't pick up a sucker. Maybe we can make some good money at that!"

"Sure we can. You just spot 'em and tell me who and where. I'll do the rest."

"Say, how about letting me have a little against my cut? Come on, honey, I'm just dying for a little of you right now. You look so beautiful sitting there. I don't think I can stand it!" Frances laughed and stretched her tempting body. Shorty got a glimpse of the valley between the succulent mounds of her breasts. His mouth was watering.

Frances had that four dollars in the back of her mind. She figured she might as well relieve Shorty of that small amount. Something was better than nothing. Shorty's feet moved him toward her unconsciously as he stared. Frances let him have a peek at one of the pink points of her breasts and saw him practically melt in his shoes.

"Honey," he pleaded, "jus' lemme kiss 'em a little, please? Jus' a little?"

"Four bucks' worth?"

Shorty pulled out the money and dropped it on the sofa beside her. She sat up and let the blue robe fall from her white shoulders to her midsection. With a lunge Shorty buried his pinched face among the soft, creamy mounds. She lay back with arms outstretched beyond his head and laughed and counted the four dollars.

"You got four minutes," she said. "Four dollars for four minutes. And don't bite!"

CHAPTER TWO

Harry Baker was one of the men who was streaming throagh the gate at the Norfolk Naval Base. Every one of them seemed in a hurry to get outside that big wide gate. They'd been at sea a long time. Now the Fleet was in, and the men were raring to get their feet on some solid ground, their knees under a bar somewhere, and their hands on a good–looking babe.

Harry walked with a big white duffle bag slung over his shoulder. He was getting out of the Navy for good. Four hitches were enough for any man, he figured. After all that time at sea he wanted some time on the beach. Harry was a tall, slim man with curly black hair and tanned face. Although thirty–three, he moved with the easy grace of a man ten years younger, and the heavy duffle bag seemed not to bother him a whit.

Harry shouldered his way through to the street. The place was a bedlam of sailors. It seemed there were at least a million of them. That's the way it was when the Fleet came in. There was so much noise you couldn't hear yourself think. The loud hum of voices and automobile horns and "Hey, Mac's!" sounded like some kind of three–ring circus.

There was a long line of passenger busses lined up along the street, with sailors pouring in them. This was not for Harry Baker though. He dropped his bag to the sidewalk and looked about for a cab. He was through with all that standing in line and being crowded in. No sir, no more of that for him! He was out, out for good, and he was going to live iike a human being again! Standing there looking for a cab, he patted the bulge of the wallet in his pocket. **It** made him feel good just knowing it was there. It gave him a feeling of confidence and future security. That wallet contained his stake. All of Harry's severence pay and his poker winnings, no small amount in itself. He smiled, touching the wallet. There was enough dough there to carry him for a pretty good little while.

It was going to have to take care of him until he could get his ducks in a row and find himself a job and get going. Once he had a job he'd be okay. He figured he'd settle down right here in Norfolk. He'd been here before on a short leave. The place was always buzzing with activity and he liked that. He had get to talking with an automobile salesman in a beer joint and the salesman had told him the car–selling business was always good around Norfolk.

Harry liked that kind of talk. He liked automobiles. All the time he was in the Navy he thought about sell ing cars when he got out. That was the one thing that appealed to him. That was a job where a man had a lot of freedom. No stuffy office to be cooped up in. A guy could get out and around a lot, selling cars. Good money to be made at it, too, if a guy worked hard at it and kept his eyes and ears open. No use going back to his old home town back in Tennessee. Too small. No opportunity, no opportunity at all. He sure as hell didn't want to get himself stuck off in a little bump in the road like that. Going back there could be the biggest mistake of his life. Hell, he wanted to get himself established where something was going on. He wanted to make himself some serious dough, not peanuts. And Norfolk looked like the place to do it.

Harry threw up his hand and whistled. A cab was just swinging in to the curb. The driver saw him and pulled up. Harry opened the door and shoved his duffle bag inside and then followed it. "Uptown," he said. The driver, a short little guy with a pinched face, said, "Okay, Mac, but I gotta pick up some more fares. Upton is too far and the overhead is too high. Us cabbies always wait to pick up a load. It's the only way we can make it. Won't take long though. Now that the Fleet's in there'll be plenty guys wanting a fast trip to the city, You don't mind, do you?"

"I do mind," Harry said. "I been around sailors so damned much I hope' I never see another one as long as I live! How much you get a head? How many you carry?"

"I carry four at least at fifty cents a head."

"Two bucks. Step on it, then. You got yourself a load and a buck tip. I don't want any company."

"Sounds like you're kind of fed up with the Navy, Mac. Have a tough trip or something?"

"No tougher than usual," Harry Baker said. "I just made my last trip. I'm out for good. Got my discharge papers all signed, sealed and delivered. I've had all of that man's navy I want. I'm on the beach for good. No, the reason I want this cab all to myself is just because I'm trying to get away from the Navy. Understand? I don't even want a bunch of the guys in uniform in here with me to remind me of the Navy. Get what I mean? I'm out and I want to get away from it, all of it."

The short driver grinned. "Sure, I follow you. I never been in the Navy myself, but I think I know how you feel. You got a stomach full."

"Yeah, that's it. I served four hitches. Way I see **it,** that's enough Navy for any man. From now on I'm a civilian . Plan to get me a job and stay on the beach. Live like a human being for a change."

"Where's your home? You talk like you was from somewhere 'way down South."

"Tennessee, but I don't think I'm going back there. Thought I might stick around Norfolk awhile and see how I like it. I been here before and I kind of like the place."

"Most sailors don't like Norfolk," the cabbie said. "They say it's the worst port in the States. Claim there's nothing to do."

"Yeah, well I guess that's right," Harry said. "But I never felt that way about Norfolk myself. I never been here but a few times but it always suited me okay. I had plenty fun in Norfolk, *especially* down there on Main Street."

"Yeah," the short man said, "Main Street is the place to have a time, all right. Find anything you want right down there on little old Main."

"They still got that burlesque? I've sure as hell seen some hot shows in that dump. You know, they used to have some damned good–looking strippers."

"Yeah, it's still in operation. They have some good girls now, too. I saw a little babe put on a show the other night that'd make your eyes pop out. Man, I'm telling you, that little babe could make that thing talk!"

Harry laughed. This brought back memories. "Roy, I never will forget one show I saw. There was this beautiful stripper, see, and she had this cat on the stage with her and she'd wiggle her tail a little and stretch out on a sofa they had on the stage and hold out the cat and say, 'Don't you love my pussy? Don't you wanta play with my pussy?' Boy, I'm telling you, she had that place in an uproar."

The short man grinned. "Say, that's pretty good. I must've missed that one. Yeah, I sure would of liked to of seen that. That sounds real good." Harry changed the subject. "Where'd be a good place for me to leave my bag? Any lockers on Main? I want to dump it and go find myself a few beers, and I sure as hell don't want to have to tote that bag everywhere I go."

The driver man nodded his head affirmatively. "Yeah, I'll run you by there. It's a clothing store. They sell uniforms and gear and rent lockers to the boys. You planning on doing the town tonight? That's what most of you guys want to do the worst way soons' you hit shore."

Harry said, "Well, I don't know. I'm gonna have some beers. If I run

15

into a good–looking babe I might work up to a shack job. I sure as hell need a babe, that's for sure. Say, is the Black Diamond still open? I had pretty good luck there last time."

"Yeah, just like always. Hasn't changed a bit. That's a good place to find a babe, okay. Plenty of 'em hang out at the Black Diamond."

"You say that place where the lockers are sells clothes? Do they sell civvies? I can't wait to get out of this monkey suit and into some civvies,"

"Yeah, they sell civvies, In fact you can buy just about anything you want in that store if you got the dough."

"Oh, I got the dough, all right. Got my severance pay plus some money I won playing poker,"

"Good," the driver said. "But take it from me, don't go get all loused up and throw it all away on a binge."

"Not me l" laughed Harry, "I been around. No, **sir,** I'm not fixing to let my little old roll get away from me, It's gotta hold me 'til I get a job and get my feet set on solid ground."

"What you planning on doing?"

"Oh, I figured I'd try to get a job selling cars, Al ways had a feeling I could sell 'em."

"They say the car business is a good racket, One thing for sure, it's something every son–of–a–bitch and his mother wants, Seem's like everybody has to have a car these days. Folks just won't walk nowhere. They gotta drive. I know a feller keeps his family half–starved to death just so's he can drive a late model car, Beats anything I ever heard of, But that's the way some folks are about cars,"

"Yeah," echoed Harry. "Everybody wants a car, that's for sure, I remember what an old man back home told me one time, He said, 'Harry, if you ever go in business, go into something that has to do with automobiles. You'll never go broke that way. People will beg, borrow and steal in order to drive an automobile!' he said, and I guess he was pretty much right about it."

"Sure he was," said the driver, "He hit the nail on the head when he said that."

"Well, well," said Harry, "so here's good old Main Street." He craned his neck to look around. "Just the same as ever. Hasn't changed a bit."

Shorty pounded on Frances' door. When she opened it he blurted eagerly: "I got one spotted, honey. And he's loaded with dough! Just brought him up from the base." The blonde grinned. "Come on in and give me the low–down," she said. "And try to keep your nasty little mind on business for a change."

CHAPTER THREE

At ten o'clock that night Harry Baker was sitting in a booth at the Black Diamond drinking beer. he had a handsome thirst on for a long time. He was dressed in civvies, a light brown suit. Hefelt wonderful. The civvies made him feel like a human once again. lie was just sitting and watching the folks and sipping his beer. The Black Diamond was crowded. There were a lot of Navy men there, and a few women too, most of thm dogs in his eyes.

Frances and Shorty came in the door. Harry did not see them. Shorty pointed him out to Frances and then he turned and left her standing there. Frances took a seat at the bar and ordered a beer. Several sailors immediately approached her, but she shook her head at them, saying, "I'm waiting for mv date."

Harry heard her and noticed her. She was the only decent, looking babe in the joint. Several more sailors made passes at Frances. She commenced to act upset, and left the bar. She came over to where Harry was sitting. "Do you mind if I sit with you until my date shows up?" she asked, giving Harry a dazzling smile. "Those wolves at the bar won't leave me alone."

"Certainly," said Harry. "My pleasure. Please do sit down. Can I order you a beer?"

"Thank you," said Frances. "My date should be coming along any min-ute." She glanced toward the entrance as though expecting somebody. Harry ordered two beers.

"He's a lucky guy – your date, I mean," said Harry. "If I was him I sure wouldn't waste any time getting here to be with you."

"Well, thanks for the compliment. He's usually not this late. I hope noth-ing has happened to him."

"Probably not," said Harry. "He'll be coming along in a minute and bring my good fortune to an end. Ah, well, such is life. I guess I'm doomed to a lonely evening. "

"Don't you know any girls around town?"

"No, I'm not from around here. Just got discharged today. That's why I don't know anybody. Haven't had time to get around any."

"That's too bad," sympathized Frances. "Well, you'll meet some girls in a few days. A handsome guy like you won't have any trouble."

Harry laughed. "I wish I thought that was true!" "What's your name? line's Helen."

"Harry. Harry Baker."

"Glad to know you, Harry. I'll introduce you to my date when he comes. Maybe he can dig up a girlfriend for you."

"That would be a break," enthused Harry. "In that case I wish he'd hurry up!"

Frances frowned. "I can't imagine what's keeping him," she complained. "He should have been here long before now."

"Stop worrying. He'll show."

"I'm not so sure," Frances said. "He's stood me up before. This wouldn't be the first time. If he stands me up tonight I'll never have anything to do with him again as long as I live."

"Know how you feel," Harry said. "I know I sure wouldn't like for a date to stand me up. I'd get mad as hell."

"Well, I'll give him a few more minutes," Frances said. "If he doesn't come by then little Helen is going home!"

"Oh, don't say that, Helen. If he doesn't come, why can't you and I get together? No use letting the whole evening go to the dogs."

"Well, I don't know," she said. "I'd feel like I'd sort of pushed myself on you. You just feel sorry for me."

"Like hell you say! Listen, honey, this is the truth. I've been hoping all along your boy friend has broken a leg or something and can't get here. By God, I'd give my right arm to take his place!"

"We'll see," Frances said. "How about another beer? We might as well have a few beers."

"Well, all right, I guess so. It sure is beginning to look like he's going to stand me up. Oh, I despise a man like that!"

"Lucky me," laughed Harry. "I hope the lug fell and broke his neck."

"You don't mean that," she said.

"The hell I don't!" Harry said, downing his beer.

They drank beer and talked until midnight. Then the bar closed. It was a Norfolk law that no beer could be sold after twelve. By then they were both feeling pretty good. "Hell, Helen, let's go somewhere and make a night of it," Harry said. "The night's still young and you're much too beautiful for me to let you go this soon. What do you say?"

"Where would we go?"

"I'm lost around Norfolk. Don't you know any nip joints?"

"Yes, I know a few."

"Well, let's make 'em. I'd like to have a few drinks of booze anyway."

"Suits me. I don't have to be home early." They left the Black Diamond and visited the nip joints, and at two a.m., loaded to the gills with booze, they checked into the Piedmont Hotel as man and wife. As soon as they entered their room, Harry set the fifth of bourbon he'd bought on a table and picked up the phone and ordered a bottle of ginger ale and a pitcher of ice. Frances was sitting on the edge of the bed. Harry dropped down beside her and started kissing her. "You're the prettiest thing I've seen in years," he said.

"Not so fast. That bellhop will be here in a minute."

"I don't know if I can wait or not!"

"Oh, yes you can–you'd better!"

The bellhop brought the ginger ale and ice. Harry tipped him a buck, and locked the door after him. Harry started fixing drinks. His eyes were bright with excitement. He hadn't expected such good fortune to shine on him that night. But now it looked as though luck was riding at his side. First night on the beach and a good looking babe all to himself! Man, what a break! But in the back of his mind something was troubling Harry, nagging at him. He tried to keep from thinking about it. It was that old trouble of his, and it was probably going to be worse tonight because he'd been at sea a long time and hadn't had a chance to be with a woman.

He knew what was going to happen, what was bound to happen. She'd like him when he first got started, like they all did, but after awhile she'd want to quit, and he wouldn't want to quit, and then she'd get mad and put on her clothes and go home, disgusted with him.

Harry pushed away these thoughts and handed her a drink. He sat beside her, took a swallow from his own glass and set it on the table. While she sipped, he kissed her white shoulder. She was wearing a sleeveless dress. She had beautifully rounded arms. He believed they were the whitest arms he'd ever seen. His eyes moved to the swells of her breasts. It was a sight to torture the imagination. Surely she was wearing an uplift bra, he thought. No woman could have natural breasts that perfect.

With his hand he gingerly pulled forward the front of her dress and peeked inside. She held her breath. His eyes bulged—she was not even wearing a bra!

"Goddam!" he said as a surge of passion swept him. And then he was clawing at the shoulder straps of the dress, pulling them down over her arms.

She lay back laughing. "Wait! You're making me spill my drink!" He snatched the glass and put it on the floor. "To hell with your drink!" He pulled the straps down her arms, baring those beautiful pink–tipped mounds of white flesh. She laughed and didn't struggle. She couldn't. The straps locked her arms at her sides.

"You didn't think they were real, did you?" she mocked.

"My God!" Harry said, lowering his face. "I've never seen anything so beautiful!"

"Don't you bite," she said. "Don't you *dare* bite!" He resisted the violent urge to swallow them whole and at once. He caught the pink tip of one between his lips and sampled it like a delicacy. Then the other one. These samplings made his brain reel with an exquisitely delicious sensation. Then he tried to swallow them whole, tried madly. She lay there laughing.

His blood was on a rampage, his brain in a dizzy whirl of passion. She was the sweetest thing he'd ever tasted. He tried his damndest to swallow her. He went about it like a man starved. His eagerness and his madness sent a thrill coursing throughout Frances' beautiful body. This was an almost alien sensation for her. She'd had so many men in the past that none of them ever seemed to do any thing for her. But here, this guy, he was something special. His terrible, impetuous passion was reaching through to her, and her body commenced to quiet under a relaxing glow. His lips seemed to be enveloping her entirely.

She had stopped laughing now. There was only a soft smile on her face. He was pulling the dress down, down, down with his trembling,eager hands. Then the dress was gone, and her petticoat was gone, and she felt her panties being yanked over the curve of her hips and then there was nothing else but the delicious feel of his lips running over her body.

Harry was burning up. He couldn't stop long enough to remove his clothes. But he knew this was something that had to be done. He stopped caressing her long enough to stand up and snatch off his shirt and pants and shoes. Then he fell hungrily upon her again. He could feel her body growing warm and soft under his lips. He could feel the surge of blood palpitating through her veins,

"Ohooo," she breathed. "Harry, you're a dog... but I love it., ." He grabbed her up roughly and set her beautiful body fully upon the bed and rolled onto it. After a few frantic tries he plunged into the exquisite warmth of her body, then he clamped her tightly to him with his arms as though to make certain that nothing in heaven or hell could snatch her away.

Holding her as tight as he could in his trembling arms, he moved his lips toward hers. She opened her mouth wide, He placed his on hers. They locked together like magnets. Then their entwined bodies began making slow, undulating, maddeningly wonderful motions,

This is heaven, Frances was thinking. And one thing is for damned certain, I'm going to have all I want before I slip the mickey in his drink.

Harry was thinking too. He was hoping this would last forever.. ,last forever... last forever and ever... and.......

CHAPTER 4

Harry woke up slowly. The first thing he was aware of was that his head was trying to split wide open. He waited there a few minutes for the throbbing to quiet down a bit and then he opened his eyes and wondered where in the hell he was. Remembering came in a dull flash. He tried to move his head to see if Helen was there. The effort like to have killed him. She was gone. He commenced to suspect something fishy. In spite of his throbbing head, he got up and found his pants and looked for his wallet. The wallet was there but the dough was gone. He dropped the pants and stood there in the room trying to fight down a sickening feeling of helplessness that was coming over him. "That son–of–a–bitch l" he said. "That dirty, common son–of–a–bitch!"

He hurried into the bathroom and threw some cold water on his face and head and ran his hand through his hair several times to keep it out of his face. He put on his clothes and went downstairs, looking for the clerk. The one at the desk wasn't the same who'd been there th night before.

"Where's that other guy–the one checked me in last night?"

"He went off duty at six. Is there something wrong? Something I can help you with?"

"Where is the police station?"

The clerk told him it was only a few blocks away and gave him dtrec- tions. Harry took off. He was going to see that bitch in jail if it was the last thing he ever did! The police sergeant listened patiently to Harry's com- plaint and filled out his report and then he looked at Harry and shook his head with disgust.

"You Navy boys get me down," he said. "If we make things too tight around Norfolk you guys complain you can't have any fun and that Norfolk is the hell hole of the world. An if we close our eyes to every little thing that happens so you guys can have some fun, you get yourselves all lushed up and end up getting rolled. What the hell do you Navy boys expect us to do anyway? Nurse you guys like babies? It's really a prob- lem. We can't satisfy you fellows any way we try. It's a losing battle all around. Some times it makes me sick."

"I don't know about that," Harry said. "All I know is that that bitch Helen rolled me for every penny I had, nearly a thousand dollars, and I gotta get it back! That's all the money I had in the world and I gotta have it back!"

"We'll do what we can," the sergeant said. "All we have to go on is her description. No doubt the name Helen is a phony, but we'll get to work on it right away. Just keep in touch. We'll let you know if we come up with anything."

He didn't sound too enthusiastic. Harry left the precinct station feeling like the biggest damn fool who ever lived. Damn, he'd like to get his hands on that dirty bitch Helen, or whatever her name was! He'd sure as hell choke that money out of her, or else!

Shorty climbed the stairs to Frances' apartment and knocked on the door. She opened it and jerked him inside and closed the door and locked it behind him. She grabbed his pinched little face and kissed him with a loud smack. "Well, you did good this time," she said. "That guy was loaded, just like you said, and I took him for every cent!" The little man was all smiles.

"Yeah? That's swell, honey. How much did you get?"

"Plenty I Over four hundred!"

"Four hundred I Man, that's a fortune! That's a real haul!"

Frances pulled him over to the sofa and sat him down and perched herself in his lap. "You know what we're gonna do?"

"No, honey, what?"
"You and I are going to run down to Virginia Beach for a few days and live it up. We'll go in your cab."

"We are? Gosh, that's a swell idea, honey. I'd like that, I'd like that a lot!"

"We're supposed to split the four hundred," she went on, kissing him every minute. "But the thing to do is for us to go down to the beach and live it up, and we'll stay just as long as the money lasts. How's that?"

"Sure, that's okay by me, sugar. I'll buy that."

"I'll handle the money," Frances said. "I'll pay for everything out of the four hundred and when it's gone we'll come on back to Norfolk."

This made Shorty happy as a lark. "Sure, baby, sure."

Frances kissed him again. "We ought to get out of town for a few days any–
way," she said. "That guy, his name was Harry, might run into you around here and start putting two and two together and tell the cops and they might connect us somehow."

"Yeah, that's right," Shorty agreed. "Everybody knows I'm crazy about you, honey. That's right, some body might put two and two together and get us in trouble. Gosh, sweetheart, you think of everything."

"You have to in this business," Frances said.

The little man's eyes were bright with excitement. "You gonna treat me nice when we get down to the beach, honey? You gonna be good to me? You are, ain't you? You're gonna be good to me, ain't you, honey?"

Frances smiled. "Good to you? You bet I am! You helped me make a good haul. Four hundred dollars' worth!" Still sitting there on his lap., she opened the top of her robe in his face and clamped his head to her breasts. "You damned little runt!" she said. "I'm gonna love you 'til your eyes pop out!"

Shorty couldn't answer. With his mouth full, and the suddeness of it all, and his brain whirling like a tornado, he was only aware that he was the happiest man in the world. Frances put her head down on top of his while he nursed like a starved baby. She smiled to herself. Stupid little bastard, she thought, he doesn't give a damn how much money there really was, all he wants is love…

CHAPTER FIVE

Harry walked along Main feeling like the world had suddenly come to an end. That damned Helen had sure put him in a spot. Oh, what the hell! Actually, there was no one to blame but himself. How in the hell could he have been so stupid? An infant would have had more sense than to get mixed up with a woman on Main Street with all that money on him. Just how stupid can a guy get? Well, the money was gone, and the chances of getting it back were not worth two cents. No use crying over it any longer. He'd been taken, and that's all there was to it. To hell with it! It served him right for be ing so damned ignorant.

He came to a greasy–looking cafe and went inside. Hiis head was killing him. It was about to split wide open clear down to his heels. What a fix to be in! Damn it! He sat on a stool and ordered black coffee. "'And hurry it up, my damned head is murdering me!"

The washed–out redhead looked at him like he was something just out from under a damp, rotting log. "You don't have to be so nasty about it," she said. "You can be a louse all you want to, but you don't have to show it!"

"Listen," Harry said, "get the coffee. Just get the damned coffee and keep your mouth shut!"

"There's always a creep to start the day wrong," she snapped, but she brought the coffee.

"There, you miserable creep, and I hope it chokes you!"

He sat there and sipped the black coffee. The red head kept watching him. He wished to hell she'd drop dead. He was shaking so badly that he had to hold the cup with both hands. He was miserable. He wished that damned waitress would look somewhere else. The coffee helped his head a little. "Hey," he said, "look here a minute."

The waitress came over. "What do you want now, creep?"

"I'm sorry. I'm sorry I snapped at you. My damned head is killing me and I had to take it out on some body."

She smiled. "That's all right. What happened? You hang one on last night?"

"Worse'n that. I got drunk and got rolled for every dime I had nearly a thousand bucks!"

"Cripes! No wonder you're feeling rough. How'd it happen?"

Harry told her the whole sordid story leaving out no detail, at least the ones he could remember.

"I don't believe I know any Helen that looks like that," she said. "Probably wasn't her real name anyway."

"I doubt it, too," Harry said. He was glad he'd soothed the red–head over. She seemed to be a pretty nice dame at that, and he didn't want to leave her with her feelings hurt. "Well, I guess I better be going," he said. He dug into his pocket for a dime. Then he reddened as he realized that Helen had taken literally every last dime from him.

"That's all right," she grinned. "I'll take care of it. Have you got any friends around town?"

"Nope, not a damned soul."

"What you gonna do?"

"God knows, I don't. Hey, wait a minute, I do know a guy here. Norfolk's his home. I was buddy–buddy with him in the Navy. Name's Staley– Claude Staley. You know him by any chance?"

"Staley? No, don't believe I do."

"Well, guess I can look him up."

"Listen," the redhead said, "why don't you stick around a few minutes, 'ti! my relief comes on? That suit looks like hell. I'll press it for you if you want me to. You can't go around looking like that! You look like something the cats drug in!"

He blinked at her. "You mean it?"

"Sure. What you need right now is a woman's care. You can take a shower up at my place and I'll fix you some ham and eggs. You look like a pretty good guy."

"Well, that's certainly nice of you," Harry said.

"Forget it. I've been in some tough spots myself."

"Have you got a phone where you live?"

"Yep, I got that, too."

"Swell, I'll look up Claude Staley in the book and give him a ring. Maybe he can fix me up with a job or something. We were damn close friends in the Navy."

"Sure," said the redhead.

But the redhead was thinking: Mister, I sure hope you're gonna fix me up, too. I need it bad. I need a job, but not the kind you're after! Harry fixed her up properly later. In the years that followed, Harry kept in touch with her from time to time. She was a hell of a good kid!

———

"What I need," said Harry Baker, "is a hot babe and a cool bed."

Spady Mears laughed. "In this weather? You must be nuts. It's too hot."

"Not for that. It's never too hot for me when it comes to a babe—especially a good–looker. The weather's always right, hot or cold. You're getting old, that's what's wrong with you."

"Maybe," Spady agreed. "Yep, I reckon when I was a hit younger I wouldn't think about the weather either. But right now I'd settle for a cold highball. Damn, this weather is terrific!"

"No wonder business is so lousy," Harry said. "Who the hell is coming on the lot to buy a car, hot as it is? Hell, you can't touch one of the blamed things without scorching your hand."

The two men were sitting in the small office in the rear of Brownley's Used Car lot. A fan was blowing hot air on them. There wasn't a customer on the place. Outside the rows of cars gleamed hotly under the searing afternoon sun. Shimmering waves of heat rose from the glowing array of colors.

"I bet this is the hottest day we've ever had in Norfolk," Spady remarked. He was a small, elderly man, known for his quick humor and his capacity to drink any man alive under the table and get up and walk off laughing. Among Norfolk's automobile dealers and salesmen, Spady was known far and wide as a sort of ageless wonder. He didn't look a day over fifty, but there were those who said they knew him twenty years ago and he looked just the same then. Nobody seemed to know his true age, but some claimed that he had to be at least eighty years old. To Harry, this seemed impossible, but from the stories he'd heard of the man, he had to admit there was room for doubt. Spady was a kind of miracle man anyway you looked at him. Harry had been to parties with Spady, and he'd witnessed the fact that Spady could drink half the night away, crawl in bed with a blond and toss her about 'til daylight, get up and go to work like nothing ever happened.

"We ought to be down at the beach cooling off like everybody else," Harry grumbled. "Looks. like every other car I see passing by this place is going up Fourth"

Granby Street, heading for the beaches. everybody wearing bathing suits. That's where we oughta be if we had any sense. Cooling off in the water at Ocean View or Virginia Beach. watching all the ladies. No telling what we might run into."

"Not me," said Spady ' "You can have the beach all you want. I think folks are crazy to lay out there in that hot sand under that blistering sun getting your skin burnt to a crisp. Nossir, give me a shady spot and a cool gin fizz any day." Spady lit a cigarette. "The only time I like to lay on that sand is when I got a blanket and a babe under me and stars over-head. I like the beaches at night when it's cool. Say, did you ever try to have a babe in the water? Boy, it's the damndest feeling you ever had. Hot first, then cold. Boy, oh boy! Hot, cold, hot, cold, hot, cold! Man, you you haven't lived 'til you've tried that."

Harry grinned. "Sounds okay. Have to try it myself sometime."

"It's good," Spady promised. Harry Baker took a handkerchief and wiped perspiration from his face. He was a tall, slim man, neatly dressed in spite of the heat. He fell to thinking about what Spady had just said. Yep, bet it would be good in the water like that. Hot, cold, hot, cold. Sure, bet it was good as hell that way. He sure as the devil was going to try that next time he got a chance.

He put the handkerchief back in his hip pocket. He'd had a good oppor-tunity just the other night, he remembered. He should have thought to try it with that married blond. Shirley. Hell, she would have gone for some of that in a big way! He kept thinking about Shirley and the beach. It was about a week ago that she drove on the lot. Her husband was a traveling man, she said, and he'd told her to shop around for a later model car while he was away.

"I don't want anything too expensive," she ex plained. "Just so it's a good dependable car." Without being obvious, Harry looked her over. She was blond, about twenty–five or six. Pretty as a picture. And the skirt was just tight enough to display curves to make any man's eyeballs sweat. He got her interested in a late model Pontiac and put her under the wheel.

"Come on, let's see if you like the way it drives," he suggested.

They drove off the lot onto Granby and Harry told her to turn North.

"Just drive her all you want," he said.

"It drives nice, handles nice," she said, driving up Granby. "Sure is a lot better than driving that old car of mine!"

"Yeah, she's a nice buggy," said Harry. "Clean, too. One–owner car. I knew the man who owned this car. Good friend of mine. Believed in taking care of a car, and he sure took good care of th is one."

"Yes, it's nice," she said.

"I know what," said Harry. "let's drive to the beach. That way you can really give the car a try–out, and I'll be able to stay off that lot. I'm telling you, that's absolutely the hottest automobile lot in Norfolk! I been suffering from the heat all day. Miserable ! Th is is a good opportunity to cool off a bit. What do you say?"

The blond smiled. "You might miss a chance to sell another car," she said. "I'd hate for that to happen on my account."

"Forget it," Harry said. "It's too hot to even talk about cars, No you'd be doing me a favor, really. I been trying to get away from that place all day, but couldn't think of a good excuse."

"Well, I haven't anything else to do. Suits me if it suits you."

"Tickles me to death," said Harry.

"It is awfully hot, isn't it? I don't believe I've ever seen it quite this warm before."

"Terrible," said Harry. "Maybe there'll be a cool breeze blowing in off the water, though. Let's drive down the Willoughby end. That way we have water on both sides. Bound to be cooler there."

"Okay. It's Willoughby Beach, then." "My name's Harry."

She looked at him and grinned. "Mine's Shirley. Shirley Grimm."

Harry poked out his hand. She placed hers in his and then pulled it away. "Grimm? Honey, you sure don't look like your name. You look any-thing but grim!"

"Well, thank you, sir."

"How long did you say your husband was going to be away?"

She smiled again, and shook her pretty blond head. "Whoa!" she said. "Hold up a minute. We can't go into anything like that. I don't mind driving down to the beach for a breath of air, and to give this car a try, but I don't want you to get any wrong impressions. I'm not looking for romance, if that's what you've got in mind."

Harry laughed. "Well, you can't blame a guy for trying. Especially with a beautiful girl like you. But okay. You can relax. I'm harmless."

"I'll bet you're harmless! I've heard about you automobile salesmen. And I never heard of one being called harmless."

"You've been listening to the wrong people," Harry said.

"I don't know about that."

"You're not really afraid of me, are you?"

"No. I'm a big girl. I can take care of myself. I just think it's better to head off trouble before it starts."

"Well, like I say, you can't blame a guy for trying." "No, I guess not," she said. They rode on in silence. Harry got to sizing up this babe. would she or wouldn't she? It was hard to tell about her. He'd known plenty of them to say no when they meant yes. Oh, well, time would tell. One thing he'd learned, and that was you never can figure out a babe, They could be as emphatic as a judge one minute and change their minds completely the next. There sure were a lot of sailors ,walking along Cranby Street. Poor bastards, Harry thought. No place to go and nothing to do. Norfolk sure as hell ought to do something about those guys. Ought to have some decent joints for them to go to. Ought to have some open bars, where a guy could go and buy a drink legally. But no, not Norfolk

Come to think of it, a sailor couldn't take a drink legally in this town—nor the whole state of Virginia, for that matter. Oh, he could buy a bottle, sure, hut where could he drink it? It was illegal to drink hard liquor in a tavern—only beer. Also against the law to drink on the street. So what does it all add up to? He can buy the stuff but he can't drink it without breaking the law! Hell of a note! Poor bastards had to slip down alleys to sneak a snort of their own booze.

Now Harry and the girl were passing City Park. He saw sailors lounging on the grass under the trees in the shade. The baggy white uniforms were everywhere. No girls, just lonesome, bitter sailors away from home and not knowing what to do with themselves. Crossing the Granby Street bridge they saw the yachts tied up at the Yacht Club. A speedboat was cruising down the river towing a couple, a boy, and a suntanned girl in white swimsuit, on skis. It was a pretty sight. Harry had never been on skis. He'd have to try it sometime. Looked like fun.

"You're awfully quiet," Shirley said.

"Just thinking."

"Hope I didn't wound the great male ego."
"No, nothing like that. I've been turned down before."

"Very disappointed?"

"Kinda. I'll get over it."

"Want to go back?"

"Of course not. Let's have the ride. This beats sweltering on that car lot."
"
Well," Shirley smiled, "I don't want you to feel you're wasting your time."

"I don't. Don't worry about it."

"Do you make a pass at every girl you see?" "

"No, just the beautiful ones, like you."

"Well, that's a compliment."

" Meant to be. It's true."

"Flattery will get you nowhere."

"Just stating a fact,"

"Do you always make out? With the girls, I mean? I've heard a lot about you automobile salesmen."

Harry laughed. "A woman's curiosity! Well, sometimes yes, sometimes no. One thing, though, you never know unless you try."

"No, I guess not. Are you married?"

"Not me."

"Ever been?"

"Nope. Never could settle down long enough. Probably get hooked someday, though. Never can tell. How about you? How long have you been married?"

"About three years."

"Don't you ever get lonesome while your old man is away?"

"Oh, sometimes. But it's not too bad. I'm used to it."

"And you mean you don't ever feel I like stepping out? Playing around a little, I mean?"

"Well, I'll have to admit I've thought about it. Haven't though."

"How come?"

"Because I don't think my husband does, that's why."

"Not much of a reason if you ask me. How do you know he doesn't?"

"I don't. I just don't believe he does, that's all. I've got faith in him."

"Faith! Hah !"

"Go on, laugh. I know you think it's crazy. But I don't care."

"And him a traveling man!"

"That's right."

"I don't get it. Pardon me, but I just don't get it."

"That's all right. Maybe you will some day."

"Not me! I'd never fall for that kind of malarkey!" Shirley looked a little hurt.

"Ifyou've got faith in somebody, you trust them. That's how I feel about my husband."

"Okay. Okay. You go along dreaming sweet little dreams about faith and men being true to their wives all you want to. But not me. I can't go for that stuff at all. Not even a little bit!"

"That's your privilege."

"Sure is."

They turned left around the circle at Ocean View. Now they could get a glimpse of the water, and smell the strong salt air. The huge framework of the leap–de dip towered high above, and they watched as one of the cars crawled to the highest peak and commenced its mad rush down-ward, roaring around the sharp curves, flying over the rails as though jet–propelled, and they could hear the men in the car laughing and the girls screaming. Oh, it was a breath–taking ride, all right! The first time always scared the hell out of anybody. Hell of a thrill!

They could see the crowds milling around there at Ocean View. Thou-sands of sailors, too, trying to pick up a babe. It was a good place. They had everything there at the Ocean View Amusement Park. It was like a big fair ground, with all the rides and such. There was the fun house where the hidden blowers blew up the girls' dresses, and there was the tunnel of love, and the shooting gallery, and the merry–go–round and the hot–dog stands and all the "take–a–chance" concessions where you threw baseballs at wooden milk bottles and things like that, and then there was the long boardwalk crowded with folks wearing swim suits, and older folks sitting on the green benches watching the water and the sandy bea and the bathers.

"Certainly are a lot of Navy men down here," Shirley said. "They're everywhere you look."

"Yeah. Thousands of 'em. The Fleet's in, you know. The guys don't know what to do with themselves."

"I bet most of them are homesick."

"Sure they are. They don't know what to do with their leave time. You'll find most of them at one of three places—in an air—conditioned movie, down here at the beach, or somewhere on Main Street."

"Main Street? That's the red light district, isn't it?"

"Yeah, what's left of it. The cops have pretty well cleaned it up now. Nothing much left but a burlesque house and a flock of beer joints. Too bad. Used to be a sailor could really have a ball down on. Main. Now he just gets drunk and lands in the brig. Norfolk is a tough port for Navy men."

"Let's stop for a coke or something. I'm thirsty." "

Okay, park somewhere along here. I'll run in the drugstore and get something."

Shirley found a place to stop just before they reached the Nansemon Hotel, and Harry walked back to the business section and went in the A.B.C. store and bought a fifth of gin and then picked up a couple of limeades at the drugstore. He got back in the car and said "I grabbed a bottle of gin. It'll taste good in the limeade. Cooling and refreshing, too. Nothing better than a gin drink in weather like this, I always say."

Shirley laughed. "That's what I always say, too."

Well, that's a break, Harry thought. At least the babe was human enough to take a drink. That told him something. No, sir, you never knew about a woman. You couldn't pay the least attention to anything they said. If a guy paid any mind to a woman when she said no, he was a plain damn fool. So he was figuring if the good looking babe would drink gin with him she might do anything. One thing, that damned gin could play hell with anybody. It seemed to work on the sex glands somehow or other. He knew it affected him that way well enough. Yessir, a few drinks of gin was equal to a couple dozen raw oysters or clams, may be more so.He hoped it worked on the blond the same way..

Shirley got the car moving again and Harry spiked her limeade heavily with the gin and handed it to her. "Can you drive and hold the cup?"

"Nothing to it. Umm, this is good!"

"Hits the spot all right," Harry said.

"Sure does."

He took a long pull on the limeade and gin. It was beginning to hit bottom now. He could feel that warm relaxing glow start in his stomach and commence to spread clear through his body. Wonderful feeling, that. So relaxing. So comfortable. A sense of well–being settled over him. The world suddenly looked rosier and he hadn't a problem in the world.

Except the blond.

He took a good look at her and he began to realize how beautiful she really was and he noticed how creamy white her skin was and what a terrific figure she had, and he got to thinking that he'd be bound to have some of that come hell or high water. He tore his eyes away and lit a cigarette and held it for her to take a drag.

"Thanks, I needed that."

"Me, too." And then he said, "Well, we're almost to Willoughby. Ever been to Willoughby? Ever been to Trail's End?"

"Never have."

"It's a nice little joint. Nothing fancy. Good food and plenty of it. Let's work up an appetite and have a seafood dinner. What say?"

"I don't know if I should."

"Why not? No harm in that, is there? It's not like you were doing any-thing wrong."

"No, I guess not," she said.

"Aren't you having a good time?"

"It's pleasant enough."

"Well, it's getting late. Gotta eat sometime. Might as well be with me. Okay?"

"Yes, I guess so."

Trail's End was right at the end of the road. It was a two–story struc-ture, and looked a little weather beaten, which it was. Down below, there was a bar and booths and a nickelodeon and this was where most of the folks sat around drinking beer. Some of them were wearing swim suits and some had on fishing clothes. Cap'n Bill, the owner, was an old man in his eighties. He was also a huge man, and he still liked his beer. He had the appearance of a Dutchman with his big red nose and heavy jowls. But he was a good old guy, and everybody 1iked him and the feel- ing seemed mutual. He had a way of making you feel right at home when you came to his place.

Upstairs, things didn't get started until later, after dark. Then a com- bo started playing at one end of the large dance floor. And outside the dance floor there was a wide porch with tables going clear around the place, and you did your sitting and drinking and talking out there on the dark porch, with the breeze off the water fanning you, and lights on the water making beautiful sights, and if there was a moon you could see the bright sandy beach circling all around. That's where they went af- ter they'd eaten, up there on the porch. He'd managed to get about six drinks in Shirley, and he could tell by her eyes that she was feeling the stuff plenty.

"It certainly is pretty up here, with the water shining and all," she said. "I haven't been out to a place like this in years."

"Having fun?" Harry asked.

"I am. I'll have to admit it, I'm having a wonderful time. Thanks."

Harry grinned. "My pleasure. Doesn't your husband take you out?"

"Hardly ever. He's usually so tired and worn out when he gets in off the road that he just wants to relax around home."

"Don't you get tired of it, staying home all the time, I mean?"

"Yes, sometimes. Sometimes I feel if I don't get out and go dancing or something, and have some fun, I'll simply die."

"I don't blame you," sympathized Harry. "I'd go nuts if I had to stay in all the time—completely batty. Reckon that's one of the reasons I'm not married. Like to come and go as I please."

"Must be wonderful," Shirlev said, "to do like you want. Sure can't do it when you're married." Inside, the combo started playing.

"Wanta dance?"

"Love to." They walked onto the dance floor hand in hand, and he took her in his arms, and she pressed against him and he knew that she was finally warming up a bit, getting in the mood. The gin did things like that' to you.

At first he didn't hold her too tight, but as they danced to the soft, slow music, with their faces touching, he commenced to hold her a little tighter, and she began to relax in his arms, and he turned his face a little and kissed her softly on the lobe of her ear, and she snuggled her face closer against his lips, and he felt the thrilling sensation of knowing a partial surrender at least, and felt the promise of more to come. Harry got more drinks in Shirley as the evening wore on, and both of them were getting a little tight, and around midnight he mentioned a walk on the beach. "Let's go wading," he said. "Did you ever go wading at night? It's fun. You're a coward if you don't go with me."

"Let's go!" cried Shirley. "It sounds like fun!" So Harry got Cap'n Bill aside and borrowed a blanket, and he got a big bottle of chaser and took Shirley and the blanket and gin and chaser down on the beach, and then they walked along the beach until they were out of sight of Trail's End.

"This is a good spot," Harry said. So he spread out the blanket and propped the bottles up in the sand. He and Shirley sat on the blanket and removed their shoes and stockings, and Harry got a glimpse of the beautiful white skin of her thigh as she pulled down one of the stockings, and the glimpse did something terrific to him and he felt an urgency that could hardly wait, but he didn't want to act too hastily for fear of spoiling his chances. After a few more drinks maybe.

He helped Shirley to her feet and together they ran band in hand down the moonlit beach to the silvery water, At first the water was ice cold on their feet and he laughed at Shirley's squeals. They sort of danced along the beach together, kicking up the cold shining water, and after awhile they returned to the blanket, a little winded, but feeling wonderful, and they lit cigarettes and lay back smoking arid looking up at the stars, and then he rolled over and laughingly gave Shirley a quick kiss, and she laughed too and pushed him away, and then he took the paper cups and mixed some of the gin and ginger ale and handed her one, and they smoked and sipped, feeling the cool ocean breeze on their bare feet and legs.

Harry had really slugged the drink he'd fixed for Shirley, and now she was humming a little tune. He felt she was bound to be pretty tight by now because she wasn't noticing how the breeze had blown the skirt high up her lovely white legs, and he watched them hungrily and longed to get his hands on her.

He restrained himself a little longer, and then he couldn't wait, so he leaned toward her outstretched body and placed his lips full on her mouth. Shirley parted her lips under his and they remained like this for a long, long time, and Harry tasted the sweetness of her mouth, soft, full, yielding, and he placed his fingers lightly on her chin and pulled slowly downward and he felt her soft sweet lips parting more under his until her mouth was wide open, and gradually he touch ed her tongue with his, and she made a little struggle, but he held her tightly, and she became quiet again, except that the points of her breasts were rising and falling rapidly, and she gave him the complete freedom of her mouth in a sort of helpless surrender that filled him with ecstasy.

She caught his hand when he clasped the silken smoothness of her leg, but he held on to what he'd gained, and finally her hold on his wrist weakened but remained there as he caressed that wonderful flesh, and the thrill of the touch shot up his arm into his brain and set him on fire. And he knew she could feel this fire through the tremor of his lips on hers, and suddenly she twisted away and sat up.

"We shouldn't have done that," she murmured.

"Why not?"

"It isn't right."

"Who says so? Anything that good is bound to be right."

"But I'm married. You're not. That makes a difference."

"Aw, hell, who's gonna know? Come on, lay back down. No harm in a little harmless necking. Come on."

"I think we'd better go," she said. "What the hell are you afraid of?"

"I don't know. I just don't feel right about it."

"Don't you like me?"

"That's just the trouble—I like you too much. It scares me."

"Here, take another drink. I'm going to have one."

"Well, just one more. Then we've got to go."

"Okay, okay, if that's the way you want it." Harry poured her another stiff one. He double–slugged it this time. He handed her the cup and they sipped along in silence. After awhile he said, "Let's take a dip." Shirley looked at him and laughed.

"Are you crazy?"

"No, I mean it. You're yellow if you don't take a dip!" Suddenly he laughed and grabbed her and pulled her back playfully and reached under her skirt and grabbed her panties. "Come on, let's take a dip. If you don't, I'm going to throw you in the water with your clothes on. How'd you like that!"

Shirley was laughing now and trying to keep him from tugging at her panties. "You're the craziest man I ever saw, Harry! Let go of my pants, you damn fool! Let go!"

"I will not! We're going swimming! How do you want it, with clothes or without?"

"You wouldn't!" she squeal d. "Harry, you wouldn't!"

"The hell I wouldn't!" He started to pick her up. "Last warning! Make up your mind!"

"I can't go in naked, you fool!"

"So what? You can wear your bra and panties."

He didn't wait for her to answer. He pulled her blouse up over her head and, holding her, started unbuttoning her skirt. She stopped struggling.

"All right, all right," she laughed. "I give up. Turn your head while I get out of this skirt."

Harry grinned in her face and kissed her. "I will not turn my head. You're beautiful and I don't want to miss a thing! Not one little thing." So she stood up, turned her back to him and dropped the skirt. The instant it hit sand, he grabbed her a round the hips and tumbled her back into his lap and held her laughingly and kissed her shoulders and made little grabs at her breasts, all in fun.

"You're crazy!" she said. "You've got a thousand hands!"

"When it comes to feeling you, Baby, I wish I had a million!" Then Harry let her up and he stripped down to his shorts while Shirley was racing for the water, He was behind her like a flash, and as she paused at the edge of the water, he picked her up and dashed out into the surf, and she yelled,

"It's cold, it's cold! Oh, Harry, don't drop me in all at once!"
Her soft white arms were wrapped tightly around his neck and he
teased her by threatening to douse her, and finally he lowered her gradually into the water, and after the first shock of cold passed, the water
felt wonderful and they swam along together. Harry lay on his back and
floated awhile.

"I never could float," Shirley said. "It makes me mad. It looks so easy,
but my feet always sink right to the bottom."

"Nothing to it," Harry assured her. "All a matter of relaxing. Here, I'll
show you." He put his hand under her back and made her lie out straight.
"Now just relax and keep your back slightly arched and hold your breath.
When you need to breathe, do it quickly. The air in your lungs helps keep
you up." Shirley lay there trying to do as he instructed. The moonlight
glistened on her lovely alabaster skin. There in the water her skin felt
smoother than the softest silk. Water had a way of making it feel that
way. Shirley lay unmoving. Harry was suddenly and thrillingly aware of
all that beauty before him, bare inches below his face, and a consuming
desire for her swept him almost senseless, and he leaned forward and
ran his lips across her belly.

"Stop, Harry! That tickles." She said, sounding forecful and convincing
But now that he'd tasted her, he didn't want to stop, couldn't stop. He
passed his lips down the length of her graceful thigh. "That tickles, Harry!
Stop it now!" It was too late to stop.

Harry moved his other hand and jerked loose the bra, and caught his
breath at the pointed beauty of her breasts. Shirley cupped them with
her hands, but he was rough now in his desperate need, and he tore her
hands away and pinned them behind her back and his mouth captured
the breasts one after the other, and then she was clamped against him,
upright, her head nestled on top of his, her hands clasping the back
of his head, and he madly kissed the beautiful rose tipped breasts as
though he could never stop, and her hands were trembling against his
scalp.

"Oh, Harry," she whispered, "I can't stand this. It drives me wild to have
my breasts kissed. That's my weak spot. It makes me so passionate
I can't breathe!" Harry didn't answer. Now he was carrying her to the
beach. He knew and she knew the inevitable was going to happen. Nothing could stop it, nothing. He laid her on the blanket and grabbed the
elastic of her pink panties and slid the garment down over the entrancing
curve of her snowy hips, down over the firm lusciousness of her beautiful
legs.

She whispered weakly, "Stop it, Harry! Please don't. Please!"

"Too late!" he said gruffly. "I'm going to have you. All hell and heaven can't stop me! And you know it, so don't try!" Now he held her arms as she struggled faintly, and took his time kissing the lovely body all over, returning again and again to the mounds of her breasts because he had found this made her moan with ecstasy.

After awhile she lay there beautiful in the moonlight and her body had grown warm, soft and glowing under liis lips, responding to them with a welcome eagerness, and her hands were on his face, on his ears and he could see her mouth open wide, and he pressed his mouth on the fulness of hers, and they fused together on meeting. Harry's blood turned to red–hot fire in his veins, and she cried a little "Oh", but he couldn't help himself, she was so good.

Then her arms locked about his neck, and his arms clamped around her body and the experience was so wonderful he felt he'd like to die right then and there, but he didn't die, and it was so thrilling to them both that they rolled and twisted, their bodies plunging to gether, and Shirley was murmuring, "Oh God, oh God," and Harry whispered breathlessly, "Beautiful, beautiful, I love you, I love you!"

"Wait a minute," Shirley said suddenly. "Oh God, wait a minute!" He held it, not budging. After awhile, she said, "All right." He started again.

"Let's make it last," he said, "we've got all night."

"All right," she answered, "all right."

So the wonderfully sweet, delicious moments ticked away to the beatings of their hearts, and the moon and stars sprinkled their entwined, rapturous bodies with lovelight, and the tiny waves breaking softly on the beach sang them a song of foreverness. On into the glorious night their hearts beat together. Now fast, now with caution, and then to hell with it!

"Oh Godl oh God!" he breathed. "You're so wonderful, so beautiful, so wonderful!" And then he found her mouth again and smothered her moans with his own, and the ecstatic blackness began to swamp his brain, and he felt like his eyes were rolling back in his head, trying to reach the blackness there, and he knew he was dying.

The two of them lay there quietly smoking and gaz– ing up at the millions of stars. "Good, huh, Shirley?"

"Heavenly."

"Let's have another drink. We'll try that again in a few minutes, soon's I catch my breath."

"Heavens no! I've had enough for one night."

"You crazy? What are you talking about? Hell, I'm just warming up. Let's make a night of it. I'm good for four or five more sessions!"
"
Not me. I'm through."

"Honey, you can't mean that!"

"Yes, I do. I'm completely satisfied. I don't want anymore."

Almost with fear, Harry grabbed her and tried to love her some more. "You're only kidding. I'll get you in the mood again."

"No, you won't. Leave me alone, Harry! Listen, now, we've had a good time, haven't we? So don't spoil it. There may be other times."

"To hell with other times! I want you now. Right now. I feel like I could love you forever!"

"No, no more tonight."

"Here, have a drink of gin."

"Nope. I'm through. I'm ready to go home."

Harry pleaded with her, trying to cacess her, but to no avail. Shirley had turned cold as a fish, and nothing would rekindle her fire. Finally Harry sighed in resignation.

"You're the most passionate man I've ever seen, Harry."

"Yeah, I've been told. I can't help it." "

You ought to get married."

"Hell! That's crazy. I've never found a woman who could give me all I want. But if I ever do, you can bet your sweet life I'll hang onto her!"
"You mean you've never been completely satisfied?"

"No, never. Never in my life. I don't believe there's a woman living could satisfy me. When I get started I never want to stop."

"That's horrible!"

"I guess so. I can't help it, though. Every woman leaves me a little disappointed. I always keep hoping I'll meet a girl as passionate as I am–who wants me all night long. God, I'd like to meet a girl like that!"

"I'm sorry if I spoiled your evening then, Harry."

"Oh, Sweetheart, don't say that! It's not your fault I'm like I am. You've been wonderful to me and I appreciate it, honest I do. Please don't feel bad."

"We'd better go," she said and began slipping into her clothes.

A few minutes later they were walking toward the now darkened hulk of Trail's End and the car.

CHAPTER SIX

A thin scratchy layer of dust covered everything in the used car office. Its presence only made Harry and Spady more miserably hot. There was a fan, a squeaky rattling fan that seemed to blow nothing but the dust and hot air.

"Cold beer sure would go good right now," remarked Spady Mears, He was wiping his sharp little face with a sweat–soiled white handkerchief.

"You can say that again," agreed Harry. His long lean body was slumped in the swivel chair which groaned at every slight movement, and his feet were propped on the scarred mahogany desk that Brownley had picked up at a furniture auction.

"Air–conditioning," Harry said. "That's what this hole needs, about a two–ton air–conditioner." Spady stood in the open door. He grunted.

"Brownley's not going to spend money that way. He doesn't give a damn if we melt or not. Not him! Not Brownley!"

"Dealers are all the same," Harry said. "They don't give a damn about you. All they're interested in is how many cars you sell, and how much money you put in their pockets. A man's crazy to be a car salesman. No future. No future at all."

Spady grinned at the younger man. "It's a lousy racket," he said. "Why the hell don't you get out of it, Harry? You're young. You got time to get in something else."

Harry grinned back at him. "Why didn't you? When you were younger?"

"Didn't have sense enough, I reckon."

"That's a lie and you know it. You stayed for the same reason I'm stay-ing, you like it, that's all." They laughed in spite of the heat.

"It's a good job for a single man," Spady went on. "No good for married guys."

"Why?"

"Too many temptations. Too much booze. Too many women. That's why so many carmen wind up in the gutter."

Harry was studying the tips of his brown shoes on the desk.

"I can handle the booze. The women, though, they might get me down sooner or later."

"A hell of a good way to go," joked the older man. "That's how I'd like to leave this old world–right smack a–top a gorgeous blond. Man, that would be The End!"

"No kidding," said Harry, and the older man could see he was trying to be serious. "The babes worry me a lot."

Spady squinted at him. "Like how?"

"Well, to tell you the truth, Spady, I never met a girl or woman who could leave me satisfied. Go on, laugh. I know it sounds crazy. Go on, laugh."

"You're bragging," said Spady.

"No, it's the gospel truth. Something must be wrong with me, but when I have a babe, and really get going good, I never seem to want to stop."

"Hell, who does?"

"You don't know what I mean. I never want to stop. Not just an hour, or two or three hours. I want it all night long. It's hell, and I know something's the matter with me. I've talked to other guys–they say they're good for maybe an hour, even a little longer. But for me it has to be hours on end. It's crazy!"

"Bet the girls like that."

"That's the trouble, they don't. Oh, some of them go crazy for a while, but sooner or later they have enough and want to stop, and that's the time I'm just warming up, and they get sore and disgusted and never want to see me again."

"Damn, if that isn't a new one on me," Spady admitted. "But you'll get over it after a while. You're just young, that's all. Put on a few years, like me, and you won't be able to last ten minutes. You'll only be good for quickies._Then you'll be wishing you had the old staying power back."

"I doubt it," said Harry. "I'm sure there's something thing wrong ."

"Oh, you'll meet a girl one of these days, Harry, who'll make you yell 'Uncle!'. That's your trouble, son, you just haven't met the right girl yet. Wait and see. Yessir, there's a woman somewhere in this old world to satisfy every man. All he has to do is find her. You'll see!"

"I been looking," Harry admitted. "I been all over the world looking. I'm ex–Navy, you know, and I been places. But I never found a babe who could give me the satisfaction I want. That's the truth, Spady, no kidding!"

"You just mind what I say, son. One of these days a pretty little thing will come bouncing along and she'll pin your ears back proper."

Harry shook his head. That would be the day! "Damn, it's hot!" griped Spady Mears. "Nobody
coming on the lot to buy a car on a day like this. What we need in this place is a shower so we can cool off once in a while, and wash some of this dust and grit off."

."Yeah," Harry agreed. "That'd help all right." The telephone rang. Spady answered it.
"It's for you, Harry. Claude Staley, I think." Harry took the phone.

"Hi, Claude, what's cooking? How's the boy?"

"Fine, Harry," said the voice on the other end. "Say, Harry, how about going along with me and Cora tonight? We're just going to knock around and have a few drinks. What say, old buddy?"

"I don't know, Claude. I sorta wanted to do something else tonight. Something more exciting. You know."

"Aw, hell, Harry, come on. Do you good not to go catting tonight! Come on, spend a quiet evening with me and Cora."

"Cora doesn't want me tagging along with you folks, Claude."

"Sure she does! She's all for it. Told me so her self."

"Well, okay, Claude. I'll drop over to your house about eight. Okay?"

"We'll be looking for you, Harry. Glad you can make it." Harry put down the receiver.

"Claude sure has a beautiful wife," said Spady.

"Yeah," Harry said. "They don't come any prettier than Cora."

"Wonder how he ever got her? Fat as he is?"

"Aw, Claude's a good guy. He and I were m the Navy together. He wasn't always that fat."

"They say he's got money."

"Yeah, Claude's loaded."

"How come he wants you tagging along?"

"Well, Claude's a heavy drinker, you know. I think the main reason he wants me along is to get him home if he gets drunk, which he nearly always does."

"You haven't been messing around his wife, have you, Harry?" Spady grinned suspiciously.

"Me? Hell, no! Not that I wouldn't like to. But Claude is one of my oldest and best friends. I wouldn't want to double–cross him. In fact, that's one of the reasons I hesitate to go out with him and Cora. She's so damned beautiful I'm afraid I might make a pass at her in spite of Claude. That'd be bad."

"Wouldn't bother me," said Spady. "If she'll play, she'll play. If not you, then somebody else. What's the difference?"

"I doubt if she'd play," said Harry. "At least I don't think she would. I haven't been around her much, but I think she's pretty straight with Claude."

"Hell," said Spady, "I never saw one wouldn't play. Not if the time and place is right. Take it from me, boy, don't pass up anything. Beautiful babe like that? Hell, if you get the chance, take her. If you don't, somebody else will!"

"You've got an evil mind, Spady." Spady laughed.

"Maybe so. But I'm a lot older than you, boy. I've learned a few things about women that'd surprise you. Take it from an old hand. Don't pass up a damned thing!"

"Okay, okay," said Harry. "I'll think about what you say, teacher." Spady lit a cigarette.

"Just like that Jean Vincent," he said. "You're sure missing the boat there, boy. All I can say, you must be out of your mind."

Harry snorted. "Ahh, jail–bait. I'd like to have some of that, don't get me wrong. But she's too young. Just a kid. I wouldn't touch her with a ten–foot pole."

"Too young? You call seventeen too young? Man, that's just the right age!"

"Get your tail in trouble," said Harry. "'Not for me. No, thanks."

"Hell, that girl could pass for twenty any day!"

"Maybe so," agreed Harry, "but that doesn't change the fact she's only seventeen. Anyway, if Bill ever caught you messing around her he'd kill the hell outta you."

"What Bill don't know won't hurt him."

Hill Vincent was Jean's father. Bill was a sales man at Prownley's Used Cars also. Right then he was off somewhere trying to make a sale.

"Speak of the devil," Spady said, staring through the window toward the street. "Here comes Jean now. Man, look at that pretty little thing! Roy, if you don't get some of that I'm gonna lose all respect for you. Hell, I wish she was throwing it all over me like she does to you! You can bet I'd for-get her age real damn quick! Boy, look at her twitch that pretty tail!"

"Aw, calm down before you bust a gut, Spady. The trouble with you is you got It all in the head. I bet if she rubbed it on you you'd jump and run like a scared rabbit. You don't fool me for a minute." Harry was lying, though. He knew Spady well enough to know that old as he was, he nev-er passed up a good thing.

Spady grinned and licked his lips. "You know better'n that."

CHAPTER SEVEN

Jean came into the office, She was beautiful, no doubt about it. The dark raven hair hung to her shoulders, and her eyes were grey–green and devilish. There wasn't a blemish on the cream–colored skin of her face, and her firm young body, which moved with an insolent confidence, was a sight to quicken the pulse.

"Hi!" she said. "Dad around?"

They told her he wasn't. "He's out on a sale," said Spady. "Mentioned he might be gone for several hours."

Jean pouted her pretty red lips. "He would be! I wanted him to run me home. I've been to a movie, and it's too hot to walk."

"It's hot all right," said Harry.

"Harry, why don't you run Jean home?" suggested Spady. "I'll look out for you while you're gone,"

Jean brightened. "That would be sweet. Harry–would you? Please? Pretty please with sugar on it?"

Harry glared at Spady. "Doesn't look like I have much choice," he said. "Well, come on, let's get going."

"Don't hurry back," Spady said, giving Harry a knowing wink. "I'll take care of things here."

"Aw, go to hell!" said Harry. "I'll be right back."

"That's right," smiled Jean. "Harry's afraid of me, Spady. He's scared to death of me!"

"I believe it," laughed the older man.

"Nuts to both of you," grumbled Harry. "Come on, Jean, if you're going."

"Just you try to get away without me!" laughed the girl. "That'll never happen!" In the car, Jean said, "Harry, what have you got against me?"

"Nothing," said Harry. "What gave you that idea.?"

"You never have liked me."

"You're crazy. Of course I like you."

"Then why aren't you nice to me?"
"I thought I was," Harry said.

"Well, you're not," she pouted. "You know how I feel about you, and you never give me a notice. Don't you think I'm pretty, Harry?"

Harry looked straight ahead. "Of course I do. I think you're very pretty."

"Then why?"

"Why what?"

"You know," she said. "Why don't you take me out or something."

"You're too young."

"I'm almost twenty."

"Hah! That's a lie. You're just seventeen. Your dad told me. So quit lying."

"Oh, he would! Dad has to spoil everything!"

"You shouldn't say that. Bill's a good guy."

"Well, you know what I mean." They rode on in silence.

"So you think I'm jailbait?" Jean smiled. Harry laughed.

"That's about it. You teenagers today are sure hep, though, I'll say that."

"You don't have to be afraid of me, Harry. I know the ropes."

"Maybe you just think you do," said Harry. "You're not old enough to know much."

"That's what you think!"

"Okay,' okay, you know it all."Hlarry shifted uneasily. "Listen," he said. "Let me put you straight on something. Guys my age don't go out with girls for just a little harmless necking. That's for you young squirts."

"So?"

"Well, guys like me want something more. You'll understand when you get older."

"So?"

Harry shifted again, uncomfortably. "Well, what I'm trying to say is, if we went out together, something serious might happen. You're a very beautiful girl, and I'm only a man. I might get all excited and do something to you. You understand?"

"Yes."

"That'd be bad. Real bad."

"Bad for who?" Jean asked. "You?"

"No, dammit, you! It'd be bad for you!"
"Why?"

"Well. .. oh, for crying out loud. I give up!"

"You mean you think I might get in trouble and name you and get you tossed in the hoosegow?"

Harry turned to stare at the girl. She grinned. "You don't have to worry about me, Harry. I've been around. I know how to take care of myself."

"You mean you've had a man?"

"No, not a man. I've let several boys, though. That is one of the reasons I'm after you, Harry. You're a man. And a man is what I want. You, Harry. You are the man I want!"

Harry was dumbfounded. "Why me? Why pick on me?"

"I can't answer that," she said. "But you're the one I want. I've been crazy about you since the first time I saw you."

"Puppy love," said Harry. "Some kind of crazy puppy love."

"That's not so!"

"Sure it is. Hell, I'm twice as old as you! You ought to go with boys your own age."

"'Those jerks? They act like children! They're anxious enough, but they don't know anything, really. I want somebody· more mature, someone with experience."

"Well, you'll have to pick on someone else," Harry said. "I'm out. But definitely!"

"Why? Wouldn't you like to make love to me, Harry? Tell the truth."

"Of course I would. Oh, hell, of course I would! I'm only hu,an. But like I said... "
"You're scared."

"That's right. I'm yellow as hell. Underage girls are dynamite. Pure and plain dynamite!"

"But you do think I'm beautiful?" Harry groaned.

"More than that, goddammit! I think you're gorgeous I'd give my right arm to make love to you. But I'm yellow. Now you know! Now are you satisfied?"

Jean smiled. "No. I'm going to have you, Harry. I'm going to have you for my very own!"

"Damned if that's so!"

''Yes I am.''

"Like hell!"

"Oh, I know how to get men. I know what they like."

"Yeah?"

"Yeah."

"Well, it won't work on me, whatever it is you have in mind. So don't try."

"You just wait and see," Jean laughed. " listen, you haven't got a chance. I'll change your mind before I'm through ."

Harry wondered what she was planning in that crazy teenage mind. Little devil, he thought, she is sure full of ginger and spice. Damned crime she wasn't a few years older. He wouldn't waste any time then. But now he had to be careful. She was tempting, awful tempting, but he'd better go easy. Could be plenty of trouble here. John Law threw the book at you for messing around with under–aged girls. Too bad. The young ones could be so tempting. So fresh and beautiful and vivacious. But that's the way it goes. Forbidden fruits. You want most what you can't have.

"Thinking of me?" Jean asked. her eyes sparkled.

"Maybe."

She leaned into the corner on her side and swung her knees onto the seat between them. Her skirt lay several inches above her knees. Harry stared, just watching

"Pull your dress down," he said. "You wanta make me wreck this car?"

"If you did, at least I'd know you like to look."

"Whal the hell—what are you trying to do?"

"I'rn chasing you," she laughed.

"Well. it's not funny!"

"Why? Don't you like my legs?"

"On hell! Of course I do. That's just the trouble. I like 'em too much."

"Everybody says I have pretty legs."

"Sure you have. Look, lay off, will you? You keep acting that way and no telling what might happen. I don't want to get excited over you. Pull that damn dress down!"

"I won't. If you don't want to see my legs, pull it down yourself."

"All right, you nit–wit, I will!" Keeping his eyes on the road, Harry fumbled his right hand toward the skirt. His hand lay on the firm smoothness of her leg. He moved upward to reach the skirt. It didn't seem to be there. He moved farther. The feel of her young flesh sent delicious shock waves up his arm. Then, breathing harder from the excitement building inside him, he felt the skirt fall over the top of his hand. One part of his brain demanded that he remove his hand. The other part wouldn't respond.

He had hesitated too long. Now she slumped down and pushed herself practically in his lap. He couldn't take his hand away for the life of him. Jean put her hands over her face.

"Please, Harry," she urged breathlessly. "Please!"

"Oh, hell," Harry moaned, "Here I go again!"

Harry told himself he must be out of his mind. But what could a guy do? He couldn't help himself. He was human, dammit! And Jean was beautiful. What man could resist touching her? Especially the way she acted? A man can't stand but so much. And when something like Jean came along and threw her beauty at you, what could you do? He bet there wasn't a man living who wouldn't fall all over her.

Her hands still covering her face, she moaned with delight, and a few seconds later she uncovered her face and grabbed his wrist with both hands. "Oh, Harry!" she said breathlessly. "Oh, I'm so embarrassed."

Harry thought Damn! This chick's hotter'n a fire cracker' He looked at her. Meeting his eyes, Jean's face turned crimson with shame. "I'm so ashamed of myself."
"You needn't feel ashamed," Harry told her softly. "Just let yourself go. Don't mind me. I know how it is. Go ahead and have yourself a ball."

"Thank you, Harry. Oh, thank you!" And she had herself a ball

CHAPTER EIGHT

Harry drove around aimlessly. He couldn't bring himself to take her straight home. He had to have some of this, jailbait or no jailbait. Hell, he couldn't stand to pass up the chance! He'd never seen a girl like Jean. Just look at her! She was going crazy, just from this. He bet she could be terrific! He thought about taking her up to his apartment. That would be taking an awful chance though. No, he'd better not try that. The best thing would be to get her clear out of town where they wouldn't be seen, by any one who knew them.

He'd hate for Jean's father, Bill Vincent, to suspect he was fooling around with her. That would be curtains! Bill Vincent was a quiet sort of guy, but rumor had it that he had a murderous temper when riled. Harry shuddered at the thought. Bill was a big, square–framed man. He looked like the kind of guy who could whip his weight in wildcats. Harry knew one thing. He didn't want to find out! He didn't want Bill Vincent out looking for him!

Harry didn't know where to take the girl. Maybe she had some ideas. He said softly, "Jean, do you know any place we could go? Now, I mean?"

Her eyes were closed and her face was flushed. "I–I don't know. Anywhere you want. Go anywhere. I don't care ."

"How soon do you have to be home? We'd have to get away from Norfolk."

"I don't care if I never get home," she said.

"We could drive over to Hampton or Newport News and go to a hotel."

"Anywhere, Harry. I'll go anywhere with you."

"That's it, then," he said. "Newport News. Nobody will recognize us over there."

Just then Harry heard a horn blaring behind him. He glanced in the rearview mirror. It was Bill Vincent! Harry jerked his hand away from the girl. "Sit up, quick! Bill's right behind us. Get up, get up quick, for God's sake!" Jean straightened up in the seat. Bill pulled alongside and motioned Harry to stop. Harry slowed to the curb. Bill stopped ahead of them, got out, and walked stiffly back.

"Hello, Bill," Harry said. "Howsa boy? Jean asked me to drive her home. It was so damned hot we decided to cruise around a bit and cool off."

Bill ignored Harry. "Get out of that car, Jean! I'll take you home from here." Harry could tell that the man was ready to explode. "Now listen, Bill, I don't want you to get the wrong idea. I was taking Jean home and that's all. Why, you don't think for a minute that I'd..."

"Shut up!" Bill snapped. "I wouldn't trust you around a baby, much less a seventeen–year–old girl." He turned to his daughter. "Go get in my car, Jean. You know I told you never to be alone with any of the men at Brownley's–and especially not with Harry Baker here!"

Jean said, "Oh, I wish you'd quit treating me like a kid. I know what I'm doing."

"Never mind that," Bill said bluntly. "You get out of there and get in my car. Right this minute!" Jean did as she was told.

"Harry," Bill glared, "you keep away from my daughter! I'm warning you. If I ever catch you with her again I'll kill you with my bare hands! That's a promise!"

Harry was pale. "Okay, Bill. Okay. Keep your shirt on. I wasn't trying to make her if that's what you think... "

Bill Vincent walked off and left Harry talking to himself. Harry watched them drive off. Whew! he thought. That was close! Well, just goes to prove it's dangerous to mess around with a teenager. Dynamite! Probably a good thing Bill spotted them and put a damper on his plans. Otherwise, he might have gotten himself in more trouble than he could handle. Damn, he must have been out of his mind thinking about shacking up with that girl. His tail would have landed in the hoose gow sure as blazes!

He'd heard that Bill Vincent didn't trust anybody as far as sex was concerned. Bill's wife had run off and deserted him soon after Jean was born. Bill had raised his daughter as best he could. She was the only family he had. The way Harry heard it, Bill never saw his wife again, nor the man she deserted him for.

Maybe he thinks Jean will turn out like her mother, Harry figured. His wife was probably a passionate bitch, and Bill's afraid Jean inherited this trait from her. Too bad. You really couldn't blame the guy. He'd probably had a tough go of it raising that girl and keeping an eye on her. One thing, she sure was a hot one, no doubt about it! He bet Bill Vincent was going to have a lot of trouble keeping her away from men. Hot and young and beautiful. What a combination!

Harry hoped she'd let him alone now. He knew he couldn't resist her. If they were ever alone together god only knows what might happen.

CHAPTER NINE

Damn! She had the prettiest pair of legs a guy ever stared at. You could look at her and feel it all over. Beautiful wasn't half the word for her. She was that way from the top of her dark hair down to the tip of her smallest toe. There was something else. It was hard to put your finger on just what it was. It was something you felt. You couldn't see it. Her olive tinted beauty blinded you. You had to get off to yourself to figure out what it was about her that made her the most absolutely fascinating woman you'd ever seen. Then you'd know what it was, and you'd ask yourself a question. How could such a beautiful woman, such an angelic–looking creature, be so damned crooked inside?

Harry was having a hell of a time keeping the car on the road. He couldn't keep his mind on the driving, with what she was doing to him. He desperately wanted her to stop and felt like he'd die if she did stop. She looked at him and smiled. There was nothing he could do about it. He knew it and she knew it. Cora was torturing all sense out of him. And she was en joying his helplessness. That was the terrifying thing about her, Harry thought. She could torture the hell out of a guy and make him beg for more.

Harry dropped his hand from the steering wheel to his lap, covering her hand. He made a little effort to move her hand away. She held on. He gave up. Then she untwined her fingers from about him, inviting him to shove her hand away. Harry Baker groaned. He couldn't do it.
Cora laughed and took her hand away. Harry cringed and gritted his teeth against the desire she'd built up in him. She could see it on his face. She laughed a gain, delightedly In the back seat, Claude Staley, Cora's fat hulk of a husband, said, "What's so funny, Cora?"

Claude was still drunk. He was plopped out on the seat with his eyes glazy and his flabby face beef red. "Just thought of something funny," giggled Cora. "Harry here looks so miserable! But I suppose he does get tired of you passing out on him all the time. He has to do all the driving, and on top of that, he always has to help you up the steps. No wonder he's so miserable. I don't blame him a bit! I can't see why he puts up with it at all!"

Harry didn't say a word. "You lay off Harry," Claude mumbled. "Harry don't mind. Me and him have been buddies a long time. Nothing I wouldn't do for Harry and nothing Harry wouldn't do for me. Right, Harry?"

"Yeah, that's right, Claude," Harry said.

Cora put her slim fingers in his lap again, and he could feel himself going crimson. "You boys certainly do stick together," she said, watching Harry's face closely. "I'll have to admit that. You're about the two closest friends I ever saw." You son–of–a–bitch! Harry thought. You lousy crooked gorgeous son–of–a–bitch!

Cora smiled at him sweetly. "Let's stop somewhere for a cup of coffee," Cora suggested. "It's just what Claude needs."

"I don't want coffee," Claude said from the back seat. "I need a drink, that's what I need."

"Not tonight you don't." Yeah, thought Harry, you want to sober him up now, don't you? You've got me all worked up, hotter than the gates of hell, and now you want Claude sober before we get home so I can't do anything about it. It's just like you to think of that, you bitch!

Cora said, "Stop at the next place we come to, and let's get some coffee, Harry." She gave him the smallest squeeze. "You'd do that for me, wouldn't you, Harry?"

"Sure," said Harry. "Yeah, sure."

"See Claude? Harry knows what's best. He knows you need coffee more than another drink. Barry has got plenty of sense. He knows when it's time to stop."

"I don't know about that," said Harry.

Cora giggled. "Oh, come on, Harry! You've got lots of willpower, you know that. Nobody could have more willpower and character than you have. You could stop doing any thing any time you wanted to. Can't fool me. Couldn't anybody make you do anything you didn't want to do!"

Harry's mind was riveted to her hand in his lap. He felt a consuming desire for her entirely swamping his mind and body. "I don't have any willpower at all," He said softly, as much to himself as to her.

Cora drew away from him and laughed. "Oh, you're just trying to be modest. I know you, Harry Baker! You don't fool me for a minute!"

"Yeah, I'm afraid you do," mumbled Harry. He reached over and took her hand roughly, put it back in his lap. Cora looked at the misery on his face and laughed again. She balled her hand and would not hold him. He tried to open her fist with his free hand. She laughed again and let him open her hand slowly, let it be placed where he wanted it. Then she squeezed him with a slightly firm touch that felt so ecstatic he thought for a minute he was going to black out.

"What's so funny up there?" Claude asked. Cora twisted around to look at her husband.

"Oh, nothing. Harry was just telling me he had no willpower, and I was telling him he was just trying to be modest. You think Harry's got willpower, don't you, Claude?"

"Sure. Harry's always had willpower. More willpower than any guy I ever knew. There's nothing wrong with my pal Harry."

At the drive–in a waitress brought. three cups of coffee and left the tray on the car window. Harry handed a cup to Cora and she passed it back to Claude. "Now you drink every drop of that coffee, Claude, do you hear me? It'll do you good."

"Aw hell, I don't want any damned coffee," Claude moaned.
"You drink it just the same," demanded Cora.

Harry handed another cup to Cora. His hand was shaking so badly that he almost spilled it. Damn, he thought, that damn woman has got my nerves shot plumb to hell! She's got me so worked up I'm trembling all over. I wish to hell she'd keep her hands off me. What's she trying to do anyway? Run me completely batty?

Cora said, "What's wrong, Harry? How come you're shaking like that? I never saw you act nervous before."

As if she didn't know! "I'm all right," he grumbled. He had the feeling she wouldn't let it go at that. Not her! It was too good an opportunity for her to add to his misery.

"But you're trembling all over, Harry! What on earth is the matter with you? Did something upset you? What caused you to be so nervous?"

That female son–of–a–bitch! he thought. She knows damn well I can't answer that one. He wished he could come right out and say, why wouldn't I be nervous? You've been playing with me all night! That's enough to upset anybody! But he couldn't say it, he couldn't do that to Claude. Anyway, Claude wouldn't believe him. He'd probably beat the hell out of him for saying it. Claude was big enough to do it all right, no doubt about that. He'd never make Claude believe Cora would do a thing like that.

"Aw, forget it," Harry said. "I'm all right, I tell you. Forget it. For crying out loud!"

"But I'm worried, about you, Harry. You must be sick or something. You're shaking awful. Claude, look at Harry, he's shaking something awful."

"You feeling okay, Harry?" asked Claude. "Anything wrong? Want me to drive when we leave? I'm sober enough to drive now."

The thought of losing his place beside Cora actually frightened Harry. "I'm okay, Claude. Forget it. I'll do the driving."

"Whatever you say, pal. You're the doctor,"

"Claude, I think you ought to drive. Something's the matter with Harry. He's got a chill or something. Let him get in the back and stretch out and you come up here and drive. After all, Harry always has to cart you around. It's time you drove him around a little, isn't that right, Harry?"

"Listen, you two!" said Harry. "There's not a damn thing wrong with me I I'm going to drive. That's that!" Cora moved closer against him and put her slim fingers on his face. Her touch nearly seared him. The faint wisp of perfume from her hand nearly drove him to abstraction. He fought the craving to lock her hand against his cheek, turn his mouth into her palm, and get the taste of her slim, tinted fingers. And she knew it!

"Poor Harry," she said, running her hand over his face and against his ear. "I believe you've got a fever, Harry. You feel so hot. Claude, you simply must drive. Harry's sick. He's too sick to drive."

You dirty bastard! thought Harry. Why don't you let Claude keep his fat ass in the back?

"I said I'd drive, didn't I?" said Claude. "That's all I can say, isn't it?"

"You're both crazy as hell!" shouted Harry. "I'm not sick and I haven't got a damned fever. Now shut up, will you? Lay off! There's not a damn thing wrong with me!"

Cora put on a mock expression of hurt. "Well, don't get angry, Harry. I'm only trying to help you."

Yeah, thought Harry, ain't that the gospel truth! "Thanks," he said, "but I'm okay."

"You're sure, Harry? Are you sure you want to drive?"

"I'm sure, now forget it."

"All right," she said. "I was only trying to help. I thought if you were feeling bad you could stretch out on the back seat and put your head in my lap. I'd take care of you, Harry, I'm a good nurse."

"She sure is, Harry," Claude said. "I can vouch for that."

Harry almost groaned aloud. So that was it! She would be back there with him, and there would be no steering wheel in his hands, and Claude's back would be to them, and Claude would not look around because he trusted them both.

"Well," said Harry, "I admit I don't feel up to par, but I don't think I'm too sick to drive. Sure, I'm a little feverish, but I wouldn't hit anything. At least I don't think I would. My eyes are a bit blurry, though, I'll have to admit that. Must be coming down with the flu or something."

"Hell, if it's like that," Claude said, "maybe you'd better let me drive. I'm sober enough now."

"Yeah, guess you better, Claude. No use taking any chances. I wouldn't want to bust up your car." Claude opened the back door and started around. Harry suddenly had an idea. He was carrying a flask in his inside coat pocket. He slipped it out while Cora was getting out of the other door, and laid it on the seat where Claude would be sure to find it. Maybe Claude would get plastered again. That would make it safer for him and Cora. He found himself wishing like hell that Claude would pass out and stay out for a week. He had to get to that damned woman, he just had to! Hell, he was hurting all over! Oh, he had the fever all right. Damned right he did! That woman would give any man a fever. Burn him right up! Damned if he'd ever seen a woman quite like her! She was a devil, no getting around that. A man could get hot as hell just looking at her, so damned hot he'd feel like his eyes were going to bulge right out of his head.

He felt like a heel doing this to Claude. But he was just weak, he supposed, but it would take a better man than he was to keep his hands off a girl like Cora. Anyway, if he didn't, somebody else would. It was al ways like that. A man was a damn fool to pass up anything these days.
Still, he and Claude had been friends for so long. They were buddies from way back, even during the war. It wasn't easy to do what he was trying to do to Claude. He hated himself. He despised his own weakness. But what was a guy going to do about it? What in the hell could you do?

He couldn't leave Cora alone. Dammit, it wasn't possible to leave her alone!

The minute Claude slid heavily into the front seat his hand fell on the flask. A little shiver of excitement went through his fat. Good old Harry, he thought. Harry had known all the time he was dying for a drink. Harry knew how it was with him. No better friend in the world than Harry. Claude wondered how he. could take a drink without Cora knowing it. He didn't want to make her mad. She could get nasty as hell when she got mad.

"Think I'll go to the men's room before we leave," he said. "Got the urge."

"Hurry back," said Cora. "Harry's not feeling well, don't forget. We've got to get him home."

"I won't be long," Claude said. In the men's room, Claude drank half the flask's contents in one big gulp. Then he lit a cigarette and waited for the stuff to take hold. Then he could 'feel the hot fire of the liquor reaching into his bloodstream, giving him his strength back. A warn glow then commenced to spread throughout his big bulky body.

"I swear that helps," he mumbled. "Feel like a new man already." That Harry was all right! Leave it to old Harry to slip that flask to him. Harry knew how badly he wanted it. Nothing Harry wouldn't do for a pal. Nossir, nothing he wouldn't do for Harry, either. He thought about Harry out there in the back seat of the car with Cora. That didn't sit so hot. It didn't sit so hot, even though
he knew he could trust Harry. He knew he could trust Cora too. Oh, hell, he had nothing to worry about! Harry wouldn't make a pass at Cora, no not even if his life depended on it. Harry wasn't that kind.

Oh, he was crazy as hell about women, and women were crazy as hell about him, but Harry would never make a play for Cora. Claude remembered that he'd known Harry a long long time. Harry had never two—timed him yet. No use thinking he would do it now, was there? Hell no! No harm in Harry and Cora being together.

Claude inhaled a long drag from the cigarette. He placed it on the window sill. He opened the flask again turned it straight up and let the rest of the booze gurgle sloppily down his monstrous throat. Then he put the flask in his hip pocket, picked up the cigarette and took another drag flipped it on the floor, and put his big foot on it. He looked at himself in the mirror over the wash basin. His face was beefy red. Drinking too much, he thought. Drinking too damn much these days. Wish to hell he could cut it down. Making him too fat. Hell, he was big as a mountain. His face looked like a big round red balloon.

Why in the hell Cora put up with him he didn't know. She sure as hell could do a lot better for herself, that was for sure. Beautiful as she was, she wouldn't have any trouble. Men fell all over her everywhere she went. lade him jealous as hell seeing them ogle her. Rut one thing, he didn't show it. He didn't want Cora to know he was so damned jealous. She'd always said she couldn't stand a jealous man. Nor a possessive one. Well, she wasn't going to see any of that in him.

lie supposed he was a hell of a disappointment to everybody. Sure was to himself. Couldn't understand why Cora put up with him at all. Look at him! Rig fat slob, that's what he was. Big fat slob! No good for anything or anybody. Had a beautiful wife, yeah. Jealous as hell over her, yeah. That was a hot one all right. He never did give her any love. Not that she wanted any, from him anyway.

He couldn't blame her. Fat slob that he was. He didn't know why she stuck to him, didn't run around on him. That was a puzzle. Beautiful as hell, Cora was. Men flipped their lids over her. But she'd always been true blue. Oh, she liked to flirt some, but what the hell, what woman didn't? No harm in that, so long as she didn't go to bed with anybody.

Claude wished to hell he was a lover. Most men were always wanting some woman, Always running around after some babe, panting like dogs with their tongues hanging out. Never was passionate like that himself. Wish he was, though. He reckoned he was jealous of Cora's beauty more so than anything else. He felt proud that such a beautiful woman was his wife. Made all the guys envy him. Any one of them would give his right arm for just one night with Cora. But Cora was his! His! And she never did anything but flirt around a little. He didn't like it, he could say that, but he wasn't going to do anything about it so long as it didn't get too serious. What the hell, got to stop this drinking, –that's what! That's everything wrong with me.

Drinking much too much–damned booze. Going to turn out to be an alcoholic if he didn't watch out. Was drinking all day long now as it was. Maybe the stuff already had him, who knows? He knew one thing, he was sure as hell shaky as the devil all the time when he needed a drink. Yeah, maybe the stuff already had him. An alcoholic right now maybe. Two hundred and forty pounds of fat soaked up through and through with alcohol! Hell of a damned mess!

Getting into the back seat with Harry, Cora grinned with anticipation. This was· going to be comical, she thought. This was going to be fun. She had Harry right where she wanted him. Thought he was so hot, did he? Thinks he's such a ladies' man! Well, she'd teach him a thing or two! He'd be a changed man when she got through with him. She bet he wouldn't be so damned conceited then. Hadn't paid much attention to her at the dance, had he? Tried to keep his distance because of Claude. Oh, sure, he'd tried his best to keep away from her. She guessed that was the main reason she wanted to bring him down to size. It was a challenge to break a man down. She always got a tremendous kick out of it. Harry had been trying to hold back because of his friendship with Claude. If it hadn't been for that, he'd been after her like a dog, like the other men. Well, this friendship angle made things more interesting.

It was hard to make a man turn on his best friend, but she bet she could do it. She reckoned she could make any man do anything for her. Yes, this was a situation that was just too good to pass up. It had tremendous possibilities. She was going to really work this Harry over. She already had him ready for the axe. He was panting like a dog right now. Cora felt like laughing. You're going to sweat for me, Mr. Harry, she thought. You're going to sweat! And Cora was going to have a lot of fun.

The minute she was in the back seat Harry was after her. He pulled her body roughly across his legs and tried to kiss her lips. Cora was laughing and struggling against him at the same time.

"Stop, Harry, stop it! You're acting crazy! What would Claude think?"

"To hell with Claude! You got me in this shape you got me half out of my mind! I've got to have you, Cora, I've gotta!!! Can't help it about Claude. I'm dying for you!" He grabbed her knee and ran his hand up her leg. The very touch of her warm flesh sent a spasm of fire coursing through his veins. Cora struggled to remove his hand. Then she turned indignant.

"Stop it, Harry! You stop that right this minute! I'm getting mad now! Stop it, I say!"

"I can't, Cora. I can't stop!"

"Yes you can. If you don't I'm going to go and get Claude. You wouldn't want Claude to know about this, would you?"

Harry sobered enough to let her remove his hand. He was puzzled and hurt. "I don't get it," he said. "I thought this was what you wanted–the same as I wanted. What the hell are you, just a teaser? Get a guy all worked up and then turn on the ice? That's a hell of a way to do!"

She sat up and smoothed out her skirt. "I was only playing," she said. "I didn't know you were going to get so serious. You're trying to go too far too fast. Anyway, I don't cheat on Claude. And you ought to be ashamed of yourself, too. Claude is your best friend. He trusts you, and here you are trying to make his wife. Oh, I don't mind playing a little, hav ing a little fun, but you, Harry, you want to go too far."

"Hell!" said Harry, still trembling. "You call that fun? You call driving a guy half–crazy fun? Well, I sure as hell don't. When I get worked up like you worked me up I want some satisfaction. I don't like to get left like this. It's not natural. You got my blood pumping like a fire hose."

"I'm sorry," she said. "I didn't mean to."

"Like hell you didn't! Like hell you didn't! You knew what you were doing to me every minute of the time. You're a teaser, that's what. Just a damned teaser!"

Cora was grinning now. "Perhaps you're right," she said softly. "I suppose should have left you alone. But I thought you'd like to play a lit-tle–just a little, you understand? I thought most men liked to be teased. I thought they liked to be worked up. In fact, I've had men ask me to tease them. They were willing to settle for that."

Harry had to admit she had something there. Her teasing him had been torture, but sweet torture. Any part of her was better than nothing. "And that's what you have in mind for me? That's all you're ever going to give me?"

"Oh, I don't know," Cora said. "That all depends. I don't say I will and I don't say I won't. It depends on how sweet you can be, and whether I get to liking you enough."

"And Claude?"

"I think the world of Claude. He's my husband. But if I decided to let another man make love to me I really wouldn't let Claude stop me. I'm not that good!"

Harry was puzzled. "I don't get it. Will you kindly tell me the truth about one thing? Why in the hell have you been torturing me, teasing me along until I'm hot enough to explode? Why? I don't get it at all."

Cora said, "Sure, I'll tell you. I get a kick out of doing it, that's why. I think it's fun. Didn't you enjoy my teasing you? Come on, tell the truth now. I told you the truth, so now you tell me. Honestly, didn't you like it? Don't you like for me to tease you?"

Harry hardly knew what to say to this. It was a new angle all right. Of course he had enjoyed it. Every vibrant living second of her teasing had been pure, torturous ecstasy. To admit it to her, though, would certainly be a blow to his ego.

She looked at him silently, solemnly, then grinned into his eyes. "You don't have to answer if you don't want to," she said. "I can see it in your eyes, though. I can see the passion. You're awfully passionate, Harry. That's good. I like that. I like to see the burning in a man's eyes and know he's burning because of me."

"You're crazy as hell," said Harry. "You're a lunatic! A damned beautiful lunatic!"

She did not laugh. Still holding his eyes, she put her hand to his face. The touch sent a spasm of fire through his every nerve. She put her other hand on his face. She moved her fingertips slightly over his ears. His breathing became harder. She commenced to smile, continually watching his eyes like a cat. Harry felt himself turning crimson, His heart was pounding again, pounding right out of his body. She could feel it. Cora passed her fingertips, those soft, warm fingertips, across his lips. Slowly, antagonizingly, she toyed with his lips. his lips came apart. She touched the tip of his tongue, sending a shot of flame through him, destroying any will he might have ever thought he possessed. He closed his lips around the delicious finger. She pushed it further and further ... and then she pulled away from him quickly.

He couldn't stop now! He grabbed her hands and tried to smother them with kisses. She kept pulling them away from him. "Oh, ooo," she said, "you shouldn't do that! You don't like to he teased."

"Yes I do," he was quick to say. "Yes, I do! Don't stop now. Please! Please, Cora, for God's sake, don't stop now!" His eyes burned into hers, and then she was laughing and he was so ashamed that he buried his face in her lap.

"Please," he begged, "please, Cora!•

"No. You don't like for me to tease you."

He was half out of his mind. "I do. I do! Anything you say, anything you want! I'll do it. But don't stop now, Cora. Have mercy! Please don't stop!" He was trying to find her hands again and she was laughing and keeping them away from him.

"Then control yourself," she said. "You want to go too far too fast. It's no fun that way."

"What do you want me to do?"

"Promise me not to get too rash. If you get out of hand I'll never let you touch me again."

"I'll be good, Cora. I swear I will!"

"Will you promise to keep your hands to yourself?"

"Yes! Yes! Anything. Just keep on doing what you were doing."

"We'll see," she said, turning his head around in her lap. "Now take it easy. It's more fun that way. Slow and easy. Oh, my, your eyes are flaming. Don't forget now, Harry, what I said. If you get out of hand, if you try to take advantage of me, it's all over for good. I'll never play with you again."

She touched his lips again and Harry's mouth flew wide open. Cora squirmed and giggled with pure joy.

CHAPTER TEN

The minute Claude slid heavily into the front seat his hand fell on the flask. A little shiver of excitement went through his fat. Good old Harry, he thought. Harry had known all the time he was dying for a drink. Harry knew how it was with him. No better friend in the world than Harry. Claude wondered how he. could take a drink without Cora knowing it. He didn't want to make her mad. She could get nasty as hell when she got mad.

"Think I'll go to the men's room before we leave," he said. "Got the urge."

"Hurry back," said Cora. "Harry's not feeling well, don't forget. We've got to get him home."

"I won't be long," Claude said.

In the men's room Claude drank half the flask's contents in one big gulp. Then he lit a cigarette and waited for the stuff to take hold. Then he could feel the hot fire of the liquor reaching into his bloodstream, giving him his strength back. A warm glow then commenced to spread throughout his big bulky body. "I swear that helps," he mumbled. "Feel like a new man already."

That Harry was all right! Leave it to old Harry to slip that flask to him. Harry knew how bad he wanted it. Nothing Harry wouldn't do for a pal. Nossir, nothing he wouldn't do for Harry, either. He thought about Harry out there in the back seat of the car with Cora. That didn't sit so hot. It didn't sit so hot, even thoug he knew he could trust Harry. He knew he could trust Cora too. Oh, hell, he had nothing to worry about! Harry wouldn't make a pass at Cora, no not even if his life depended on it. Harry wasn't that kind. Oh, he was crazy as hell about women, and women were crazy as hell about him, but Harry would never make a play for Cora. Claude remembered that he'd known Harry a long long time. Harry had never two–timed him yet. No use th inking he would do it now, was there? Hell no! No harm in Harry and Cora being together.

Claude inhaled a long drag from the cigarette. He placed it on the window sill. He opened the flask a gain and turned it straight up and let the rest of the booze gurgle sloppily down his monstrous throat. Then he put the flask in his hip pocket, picked up the cigar ette and took another drag and flipped it on the floor and put his big foot on it. He looked at himself in the mirror over the wash basin. His face was beefy red. Drinking too much, he thought. Drinking too damn much these days. Wish to hell he could cut it down. Making him too fat. Hell, he was big as a mountain. His face looked like a big round red balloon. Why in the hell Cora put up with him he didn't know. She sure as hell could do a lot better for herself, that was for sure. Beautiful as she was, she wouldn't have any trouble.

Men fell all over her everywhere she went. lade him jealous as hell seeing them ogle her. But one thing, he didn't show it. He didn't want Cora to know he was so damned jealous. She'd always said she couldn't stand a jealous man. Nor a possessive one. Well, she wasn't going to see any of that in him.

He supposed he was a hell of a disappointment to everybody. Sure was to himself. Couldn't understand why Cora put up with him at all. Look at him! Rig fat slob, that's what he was. Big fat slob! No good for anything or anybody. Had a beautiful wife, yeah. Jealous as hell over her, yeah. That was a hot one all right. He never did give her any loving. Not that she wanted any, from him anyway. He couldn't blame her. Fat slob that he was. He didn't know why she stuck to him, didn't run around on him. That was a puzzle. Beautiful as hell, Cora was. Men flipped their lids over her. But she'd always been true blue. Oh, she liked to flirt some, but what the hell, what woman didn't? No harm in that, so long as she didn't go to bed with anybody.

Claude wished to hell he was a lover. Most men were always wanting some woman, Always running around after some babe, panting like dogs with their tongues hanging out. Never was passionate like that himself. Wish he was, though. He reckoned he was jealous of Cora's beauty more so than anything else. He felt proud that such a beautiful woman was his wife. Made all the guys envy him. Any one of them would give his right arm for just one night with Cora. But Cora was his! His! And she never did anything but flirt around a little. He didn't like it, he couldn"t say that, but he wasn't going to do anything about it so long as it didn't get too serious. What the hell, got to stop this drinking, that's what! That's everything wrong with me. Drinking much too much damned booze. Going to turn out to be an alcoholic if he didn't watch out. Was drinking all day long now as it was. Maybe the stuff already had him, who knows? He knew one thing, he was sure as hell shaky as the devil all the time when he needed a drink. Yeah, maybe the stuff already had him. An alcoholic right now maybe. Two hundred and forty pounds of fat soaked up through and through with alcohol! Hell of a damned mess!

Getting into the back seat with Harry, Cora grinned with anticipation. This was· going to be comical, she thought. This was going to be fun. She had Harry right where she wanted him. Thought he was so hot, did he? Thinks he's such a ladies' man! Well, she'd teach him a thing or two! He'd be a changed man when she got through with him. She bet he wouldn't be so damned conceited then. Hadn't paid much attention to her at the dance, had he? Tried to keep his distance because of Claude. Oh, sure, he'd tried his best to keep away from her. She guessed that was the main reason she wanted to bring him down to size. It was a challenge to break a man down. She always got a tremendous kick out of it. Harry had been trying to hold back because of his friendship with Claude. If it hadn't been for that, he'd been after her like a dog, like the all the other men. Well, this friendship angle made things more interesting. It was hard to make a man turn on his best friend, but she bet she could do it. She reckoned she could make any man do anything for her. Yes, this was a situation that was just too good to pass up. It had tremendous possibilities. She was going to really work this Harry over. She already had him ready for the axe. He was panting like a dog right now. Cora felt like laughing. You're going to sweat for me, Mr. Harry, she thought. You're going to sweat! And Cora was going to have a lot of fun.

The minute she was in the back seat Harry was after her. He pulled her body roughly across his legs and tried to kiss her lips. Cora was laughing and struggling against him at the same time. "Stop, Harry, stop it! You're acting crazy! What would Claude think?"

"To hell with Claude! You got me in this shape you got me half out of my mind! I've got to have you, Cora, I've gotta! I can't help it about Claude. I'm dying for you!" He grabbed her knee and ran his hand up her leg. The very touch of her warm flesh sent a spasm of fire coursing through his veins. Cora struggled to remove his hand. Then she turned indignant.

"Stop it, Harry! You stop that right th is minute! I'm getting mad now! Stop it, I say!"

"I can'.t, Cora. I can't stop!"

"Yes you can. If you don't I'm going to go and get Claude. You wouldn't want Claude to know about this, would you?"

Harry sobered enough to let her remove his hand. He was puzzled and hurt. "I don't get it," he said. "I thought this was what you wanted, the same as I wanted. What the hell are you, just a teaser? Get a guy all worked up and then turn on the ice? That's a hell of a way to do!"

She sat up and smoothed out her skirt. "I was only playing," she said. "I didn't know you were going to get so serious. You're trying to go too far too fast. Anyway, I don't cheat on Claude. And you ought to be ashamed of yourself, too. Claude is your best friend. He trusts you, and here you are trying to make his wife. Oh, I don't mind playing a little, having a little fun, but you, Harry, you want to go too far."

"Hell!" said Harry, still trembling. "You call that fun? You call driving a guy half crazy fun? Well, I sure as hell don't. When I get worked up like you worked me up I want some satisfaction. I don't like to get left like this. It's not natural. You got my blood pumping like a fire hose."

"I'm sorry," she said. "I didn't mean to."

"Like hell you didn't! Like hell you didn't! You knew what you were doing to me every minute of the time. You're a teaser, that's what. Just a damned teaser!"

Cora was grinning now. "Perhaps you're right," she said softly. "I suppose should have left you alone. But I thought you'd like to play a little, just a little, you understand? I thought most men liked to be teased. I thought they liked to be worked up. In fact I've had men ask me to tease them. They were willing to settle for that."

Harry had to admit she had something there. Her teasing him had been torture, but sweef torture. Any part of her was better than nothing. "And that's what you have in mind for me? That's all you're ever going to give me?"

"Oh, I don't know," Cora said. "That all depends. I don't say I will and I don't say I won't. It depends on how sweet you can be, and whether I get to liking you enough."

"And Claude?"

"I think the world of Claude. He's my husband. But if I decided to let another man make love to me I really wouldn't let Claude stop me. I'm not that good!"

Harry was puzzled. "I don't get it. Will you kindly tell me the truth about one thing? Why in the hell have you been torturing me, teasing me along until I'm hot enough to explode? Why? I don't get it at all."

Cora said, "Sure, I'll tell you. I get a kick out of doing it, that's why. I think it's fun. Didn't you enjoy my teasing you? Come on, tell the truth now. I told you the truth, so now you tell me. Honestly, didn't you like it? Don't you like for me to tease you?"

Harry hardly knew what to say td this. It was a new angle all right. Of course he had enjoyed it. Every vibrant living second of her teasing had been pure, torturous ecstasy. To admit it to her, though, would certainly be a blow to his ego. She looked at him silently, solemnly, then grinned-into his eyes.

"You don't have to answer if you don't want to," she said. "I can see it in your eyes, though. I can see the passion. You're awfully passionate, Harry. That's good. I like that. I like to see the burning in a man's eyes and know he's burning because of me."

"You're crazy as hell," said Harry. "You're a lunatic! A damned beautiful lunatic!"

She did not laugh. Still holding his eyes, she put her hand to his face. The touch sent a spasm of fire through his every nerve. She put her other hand on his face. She moved her fingertips slightly over his ears. His breathing became harder. She commenced to smile, continually watching his eyes like a cat. Harry felt himself turning crimson, His heart was pounding again, pounding right out of his body. She could feel it. Cora passed her fingertips, those soft, warm fingertips, across his lips. Slowly, antagonizingly, she toyed with his lips. Ilis lips came apart. She touched the tip of his tongue, sending a shot of flame through him, de stroying any will he might have ever thought he possessed. He closed his lips around the delicious finger. She pushed it further and further and then she pulled away from him quickly.

He couldn't stop now! He grabbed her hands and tried to smother them with kisses. She kept pulling them away from him. "Oh,oooo," she said, "you shouldn't do that! You don't like to he teased."

"Yes I do," he was quick to say. "Yes I do! Don't stop now. Please! Please, Cora, for God's sake, don't stop now!"

His eyes burned into hers, and then she was laughing and he was so ashamed that he buried his face in her lap.

"Please," he begged, "please, Cora!"

"No. You don't like for me to tease you."

He was half out of his mind. "I do. I do! Anything you say, anything you want, I'll do it. But don't stop now, Cora. Have mercy! Please don't stop!" He was trying to find her hands again and she was laughing and keeping them away from him.

"Then control yourself," she said. "You want to go too far too fast. It's no fun that way."

"What do you want me to do?"

"Promise me not to get too rash. If you get out of hand I'll never let you touch me again." "I'll be good, Cora. I swear I will!"

"Will you promise to keep your hands to yourself?"

"Yes! Yes! Anything. Just keep on doing what you were doing."

"We'll see," she said, turning his head around in her lap. "Now take it easy. It's more fun that way. Slow and easy. Oh, my, your eyes are flaming. Don't forget now, Harry, what I said. If you get out of hand, if you try to take advantage of me, it's all over for good. I'll never play with you again."

She touched his lips again and Harry's mouth flew wide open. Cora squirmed and giggled with pure joy.

CHAPTER ELEVEN

Claude stumbled back to the car. He. was pretty drunk again now. He was having trouble keeping his balance. He practically fell into the front seat. "How's Harrv?" he asked.

He had noticed that Harry's head was in Cora's lap. "He's still feverish," Cora answered. "In fact he's burning up."

"Yeah, he's breathing awful hard too," Claude remarked. "I can hear him breathing loud. How you feeling, Harry?"

" Tough," Harry moaned. His voice almost cracked. "I guess we better be getting home," Cora said.

"We should get Harry to bed. Can you drive, Claude? You looked tipsy coming back to the car."

"I'm okay," said Claude. "Are we going to leave Harry off at his flat? Sick like that? All by himself?"

"What else?" answered his wife.

"Well. we could take him home with us. lie could sleep on the sofa. At least there'd be somebody to take care of him if he gets worse,"

"That's an idea," Cora agreed. "How about it, Harry? Do you want to spend the night with us so we can look after you?"

"I hate to put you nut," said Harry.

"Forget it, pal. You're not putting us out. Me and Cora don't want you sick up there in your flat all by yourself. Over at our place, we can look after you."

Cora patted his cheek "Sure, Harry. We'll look after you. How about it?"

"Whatever you say," Harry said.

Claude managed to get the car out on the road and rolling. He commenced to straighten up a bit, but his brain was still fuzzy. This damned drinking was going to get him down, he was thinking. Got to stop it. Got to stop it before it's too late. Didn't know why he couldn't handle the stuff like Harry could. Harry could get drunk and wake up the next morning feeling fine. Like nothing ever happened. Wish to hell he could do that. No. He couldn't do it. Had to have a big slug before he could get going. Same thing every morning. Had to have that drink. Belly felt like it was full of ants. Nerves tight and screaming for a shot. Couldn't eat. Couldn't eat a damned bite 'til he'd had that shot of booze. Liked to take a big one, half a water glass full when he first opened his eyes in the morning, smoke a cigarette, then he'd feel a little better, and then just before he sat down to eat, he'd have to have one more. A good one this time. Not as big as the first, but a good shot just the same, to put an edge to his appe tite. This had been going on for years now.

Wonder if he was an alcoholic? They say that when you have to have the shot first thing in the morning, you're an alcoholic. Wonder if there's anything in that? Why couldn't he leave the stuff alone like Harry could? Harry drank just as much as he did, More at times. Why didn't Harry have to have a shot in the mornings?· Sure was a puzzle. Couldn't figure it out. Well, they say some men are born to be alcoholics. They say some men drink all their lives and never get to be an alcoholic, while other men get to be an alco holic in no time at all. Somebody said it was an aller-gy. They said that some men are allergic to alcohol like some folks are allergic to cats. Life sure is crazy as hell.

There he was, a big fat slob, always full of booze, and he couldn't let the booze alone, and yet he'd never had any trouble making good money. He guessed that's one of the reasons Cora stayed with him, the money, She always had money to spend on herself. He saw to that, Didn't know what she'd do if he went broke. Leave him probably. Leave him flat. Surely she didn't really love him, big fat slob like him. What did he have to offer her except money? She certainly didn't stay with him for sex. He had known for a long time that Cora was, practically void of any sex feelings. Well, he was the same way himself. He had never been right since the operation. And he'd been getting fatter and fatter. Well, it was what Cora had wanted. She wouldn't marry him if he didn't have him self cut. Didn't want any children, she'd said.

She had a horror of childbirth. He was so crazy about her back then he would have done anything. So he went to old Doc Sawyer and had himself tied off, made unfertile. Couldn't have any kids that way. That's the way Cora wanted it. Wouldn't marry him any other way. Well, if that's what it took to get her, he'd do it and did. And then after that, he started getting to be the big fat slob and he couldn't seem to stop it. Oh, he'd been a pretty big guy before, but after the operation, everything he ate turned to grease, turned to fat.

That wasn't all. He lost his appetite for lovemaking, for going to bed with Cora for that purpose alone. It wasn't supposed to work that way, it wasn't supposed to have any effect on him that way, but it did just the same, and his whole outlook on life had changed. He didn't have the old get–up–and–go anymore. He didn't have the old confidence, the cock–suredness he'd had be fore. He'd never felt completely alive like he had felt before the operation. Oh, well, it was too late to worry about that now. It was all over and done with and noth ing he could do about it.

One good thing, Cora didn't seem to mind. In fact, he was sure she didn't go in too much for the lovemaking. Cora was cold as an ice berg as far as sex was concerned. It was a good thing. If she was hot–natured he couldn't hold her a minute. She'd leave him in a second. How long had it been now since they'd really done anything? A year? More? He was mighty glad she never mentioned it. He really didn't know if he could do anything any longer. He loved her, loved her to death, but not that way. He just couldn't feel the sex. It didn't bother him a bit. One good thing, he never suffered over sex today like he did in the days before he married Cora. Back then sex had been all he could think of and he never seemed to get himself completely satisfied. This way had more contentment at least. That was one way to look at it.

In the back seat Harry made a sound almost like a muffled moan. "Harry all right?" Claude asked over his shoulder.

"Yes, but he's awful feverish," Cora answered.

"Heard him moan."

"Yes, but he's all right now," said Cora.

Claude kept his eyes pinned on the road. He wondered if the operation had anything to do with his drinking. Could be that. Just the knowledge that a man is not quite a man, and can't Have any kids is bound to have some effect on a man. He was ashamed of not being potent, he knew that. Always had been ashamed of it. I\laybe that was the reason for all his trouble. They say that too much drinking comes from a mental quirk. They say that alcoholism is a disease, a mental disease, that a guy is trying to hide something, or can't face up to something, or something like that. Sure, maybe that's it. Bet it is, bet it is. Well, he had to stop that dri king and that's all there was to it. Had to stop before he ended up in the gutter.

Oh, hell! he thought, everybody is trying to escape from something. Even Cora. Cora can't stand the thought of having a child. Her mind's screwy that way. Must have got that way when her mother died while Cora's brother was being born. She was just old enough to remember that. Probably been on her mind ever since. Probably can't face up to it. Bet that's the reason she hates her brother too. Never can tell. Crazy things happen to people in this old crazy mixed–up world.

CHAPTER TWELVE

The living room was dimly alight with moonglow. A big window was at one end, and Harry could see that the moon was so bright it was almost like day outside. He lay quietly on. the sofa staring at the big window. He couldn't sleep. He had an ashtray on the floor be side him. It was practically full of stubs of burnt cigarettes where he'd been smoking constantly. He just couldn't get Cora off his mind. Damn her to hell! She was driving him crazy! Her every feature was burnt into his brain as though etched there with a red–hot iron.

She had really put him through a tantalizing experience during the ride home. She'd worked on him there in that back seat. It was one ride he'd never forget. She had him in a kind of trap, what with Claude right up front driving the car. She had him at her mercy, so to speak. He had to hold himself in check to keep Claude from suspecting anything was going on. God, how she'd teased and tormented him I He didn't know even now how he'd managed to keep from raping her right there, in spite of Claude. But he somehow managed to hold onto his wits even though he was crazy for her.

He couldn't figure her out. She seemed to get a sadistic pleasure from torturing him like that. He liked it though. What man wouldn't? She was beautiful, and he imagined any man would like to be teased like that by a beautiful woman.

Cora was sexy. She had more sex appeal than any other woman he had ever known. She just had it, that's all. Any way you looked at her. You could feel it in the air when she was around. He wondered why some women had it and some didn't. Sure, there were plenty of beautiful women in the world. But some of them had sex appeal and some didn't. It was an elusive quality, but you knew it the second you saw it. He had known plenty of women who could get him excited just by looking at them, Cora was like that, only more so. Cora was dripping with sex appeal.

How in the hell had Claude got her? he wondered. They just didn't look right together, didn't fit some how. He couldn't imagine any woman going for Claude. Maybe it was his money, Claude always had plenty of jack. He owned three service stations now. Maybe she hung onto Claude for security. Claude was a businessman, you had to hand him that. If he was nothing else he was a businessman. He knew how to make money. He'd started from scratch and built his business up from one measly service station to three. Now he had a bunch of guys working for him. Harry didn't know what Claude could retire if he wanted to. No doubt he was loaded. But he still worked every day just like one of the help. Sometimes he'd come home greasy as a hog.

Harry smoked on his cigarette there in the semi darkness. This was a nice apartment they had. Second story job. Nice furniture. Good taste, too. He bet Cora was the cause of that. He bet she picked out every stick of furniture in the place. Thick mg on the floor. Bet that cost a pretty piece of change. Well, he thought, if she could work Claude over like she had worked on him, she probably got anything she wanted from Claude. Oh, hell, how do you know? She might not ever fool around with Claude that way. Bet ten dollars she didn't. She probably didn't even want to get Claude worked up. Probably didn't want any part of him. Couldn't say he blamed her much, big as Claude was. Who'd want two tons of beef squashing them?

You never could tell, though. Cora was a funny one all right. Never know what a crazy dame like her might want. He wondered if she really was true to Claude. Could be. It was possible all right. He'd known some other women in his life who'd play along but wouldn't go any farther. Yep, that was true. But he'd never known one who liked to play exactly like Cora. She drove you out of your mind and laughed at you. It was sheer joy to her. She admitted it. And the hell of it was she made you like it and beg for more She had an instinct for it. Knew just how to get a guy going. Just how fast or slow to work him. She got you half crazy with desire and then gave you the smallest taste just to keep your appetite whetted and your blood boiling for more.

Sure, she'd give you a taste, just enough so you'd know what you were missing by not getting more. She'd set up a craving in you all right. In the car, she'd done that to him. Played with him a sort of cat and mouse game, fun for her, torture for him, and yet he was like the insect flying around the flame, practically begging to be destroyed .... begging for more of the delicious, tantalizing torture. God, she could do things to you with her hands I Just with her hands. Just with those slim warm fingers of hers. On your face ....over your eyes ....tickling your ears ....toying with your lips, touching your tongue ....teasing....teasing teasing....until you felt like your eyeballs were going to pop right out of your head, and just when you felt like you couldn't stand it anymore, she'd see your mouth open and she'd muffle any sound you were going to make with her soft palms, and when you'd quieted a bit she'd smile and start working on you all over again. And you had to keep your hands to yourself or she'd stop and wouldn't touch you and freeze up until you put your hands down by your sides again and clinched your fists, waiting and hoping for her to go back having her fun, and after awhile you knew that she knew that she had you where she wanted you, under perfect control, and she could do what she liked and you wouldn't do anything to stop her, only lie there with your head in her lap, staring upward with the veins in your temple pounding like hell and your heart feeling like it was going to explode and not feeling any shame any more because you knew your eyes were bulging and she was watching them and trying to make them bulge even more and grinning down at you with almost childish delight ....and then ....and then she had become really cruel pushing his face sideways toward her knees, just so you could see, and holding your face just bare inches from a little gleaming spot of bare flesh just above her knees, so beautiful, so shining where the moon light fell across, and you felt like you'd die if you didn't get your lips there, and she'd almost let you, but she wouldn't quite let you, and if you commenced to struggle, she'd cover the beautiful bare place just above her knees until finally you learned not to try too hard and then she would let you taste her flesh just for a second and when your lips made contact it was so thrilling that you opened your lips as wide as you could, as though you were afraid you'd never get another chance.

In the next room, Claude was snoring loudly. Listening to him, Harry could think of a thousand possibilities. Almost anything could happen without Claude waking up. He wondered about Cora lying there beside Claude. Suppose she was asleep? Or was she thinking about him lying out there in the living room on the sofa? The last thing she had whispered before retiring was, "Think about me, Harry. Think about me a lot!" And she had laughed and left him.

Think about her! As if he could do anything else! She had burned her imprint into his brain and she knew it! She hoped to tease him even while she slept! And a good job was being done.
Harry lit another cigarette. If only she'd come to him! That was one of the possibilities. If she'd only come to him! It would be so easy for her. Claude was sleeping like a log, snoring away like a buzz–saw. Anything could happen without his waking. They'd be able to use his snoring as a warning signal. If he stopped snoring she could run back to bed before he became fully awake. But as long as the snoring continued they could do anything they wanted to do in perfect safety. Why didn't she come ... why didn't she come to him through that open door?

He found himself staring at that open door and realized that he'd had it pin–pointed with his eyes for hours maybe, hoping to see her materialize there in the moonlight. Once he gave a start and his breath froze because his mind had actually conjured up her image and he had to stare a long time before he knew she wasn't there at all and that his desire for her was so strong that his mind was beginning to play tricks.

Then it happened. A click. Like the click of a cigarette lighter. Harry's heart missed a beat. He saw the faint flare of light through the door as she lit a cigarette. His brain caught fire instantly. Was that a signal? Was Cora letting him know she was awake and thinking of him? Was she getting ready to come to him? A thousand questions raced through his mind all at once, each of them filled with great thoughts and expectations.

So she was lying there smoking. Harry felt sure she'd lit that cigarette as some kind of signal for him, had to be. Sure, he thought, she's going to come in here on the sofa with him. Then they'd have a time of it! If she wanted a loving up she'd never forget, all she had to do was get in there with him. He was primed all right. Primed to hell and gone! Perhaps this was what she'd been leading up to all night long... priming him for the time when Claude would be safely asleep and they could get together. It had to be that, it had to, there couldn't be any other reason! He lay there hardly breathing. Sweating with his thoughts of Cora slipping through that door coming

in something flimsy and perfumed ... lying on the sofa with him and letting him satisfy the craving she'd so carefully built up in him.

Oh, why in the hell didn't she do something? It was safe enough, she ought to realize that. Claude was snoring loudly and regularly. Not no chance of him waking up. All she had to do was slip easily and quietly out of bed and tiptoe into the living room. What the hell and damnation was she waiting for? Damn, he couldn't stand much more of this! His mind was ready to explode with anticipation. Why in the living hell didn't she come on?

What the hell! She wasn't doing this to him on purpose, was she? Wasn't trying to antagonize him even further, was she? Who knows, dammit, it would be just like her. That was a thought. That was just exactly what that damned bitch was trying to do! Curse her soul to hell! That crazy, scheming, conniving, teasing, tantalizing beautiful son–of–a–bitch! He ought to go in

there and yank her ass out of bed and drag her in the living room and rape the living hell right out of her! That'd teach her some manners! Son–of–a–bitch, that's just what she needed! Somebody to give her the lay of her life! That'd take some of that fire out of her!

Please, Cora, please come to me...

CHAPTER THIRTEEN

In the bedroom Cora lay there smiling to herself and watching her dressing table mirror. If Harry came to the door she could see him. She wondered if he had the nerve. Or, rather, if he had the willpower not to. She believed sooner or later he would. She had him going good, she grinned to herself. He was so hot for her she didn't believe he could resist, in spite of the fact that Claude was there on the other side of the bed, away from the door, and in spite of the fact that Claude and Harry were supposed to be best friends. This certainly presented an interesting challenge, she thought. What would be the strongest in Harry's mind, his friend ship bond with Claude or his passion to be with her?

Well, she'd see. She'd see just how much power she held over Harry. She kept glancing at the mirror. Oh, he'd come sneaking to the door all right. She knew he'd noticed when she snapped the cigarette lighter. She could follow his every thought. He thought perhaps she was coming in there on the sofa to him. Let him think it! Let him think and wait and sweat. She bet the anticipation was killing him. Men were crazy that way, she'd found. Whet their appetites a little and they were just like dogs, waiting with their ears perked and their mouths panting. Harry was a passionate one all right. Passionate as hell once you got him started. She didn't believe she'd ever played with a man who got as hot and crazy as Harry. He was a lot of fun.

She'd had herself a ball with him in the back seat of the car. If she'd turned him loose no telling what he'd done. If Claude hadn't been there she believed he would actually have eaten her up. Gee, that was fun making Harry that hot! She remembered how she could feel his temples throbbing, and when she showed him a glimpse of her knees he'd nearly gone crazy. She almost laughed now, thinking how badly he'd wanted to kiss her there above her knees, and when she'd finally let him have a taste she'd thought he was going to swallow her.

She'd sure had him excited, that was a cinch. She'd teased him until he'd have cut off his arm for her, she bet. Once or twice she'd thought he was going to cry out and she'd had to muffle him with her fingers be tween his lips and her other hand covering his mouth also, and she'd have to hold him that way until he got some of his senses back. Oh, she'd teased a lot of men in her life, but she had never known one to go as crazy as Harry. Yessir, she was going to have a lot of fun out of this. She had Mr. Harry twisted around her little finger and she was going to make him squirm but good!

Suddenly she knew Harry was in the doorway. She could feel him there, sense his presence. Then, dimly, she could see his outline in the mirror. She grinned impishly to herself. She'd known he couldn't stay away. She twisted over onto her right side and looked up at him. She smiled and laid on her stomach and reached down and put her cigarette out in the ashtray. Then she got back on her side and looked up at him again. His head was poked just inside the room.

lie motioned for her to get up and come with him. She shook her head. He bent forward, almost down to her ear.

"Please," he whispered, "please come on in the living room. "We'll have a lot of fun. Claude won't wake up."

She whispered back, "No."
"Aw, come on, Cora." His voice was ready to crack. "

No. no." she whispered. "You go on back like a nice boy and go to sleep."

"Hell, you know I can't sleep!"

"Careful, Claude will hear."

"Hell, a stick of dynamite couldn't budge him. He's out for the rest of the night. Come on, Cora, get up, let's have some fun."

She shook her head. Quietly, he kneeled beside her. "What's wrong? What are you afraid of?"

"Of you."

"Why?"

"Because you're too passionate. Couldn't handle you if Claude wasn't around. You might do something bad." Claude was snoring loudly. Cora put her hands on Harry's face and pulled his mouth to hers, and when their lips touched and commenced to melt together, she opened her mouth wide, and he did the same, and their tongues caressed each other's tongue hotly and then she twisted her head away from him, and he ran his lips down her throat slowly and across the soft spot under her shoulder, then down her arm, and following this he pulled the strap of her negligee downward, baring her breasts, but before he could get to them she covered them with her hands, and all he could find to kiss were the swells that ran off from her palms. Then slowly, antagonizingly, she spread her fingers and let him get to her nipples, just between his lips.

This maddening procedure, enhanced by her perfumed body in his nostrils drove Harry practically insane with desire.

"Stop now," she said in a whisper, knowing perfectly well he couldn't stop. "Harry, stop it!"

"I can't stop. I can't!"

But she knew one thing that would sober him. "Stop, or I'll wake Claude!"

Harry stopped suddenly at the mention of Claude.

"Why are you doing this to me, Cora? It's inhuman."

"It's fun."

"You're cruel as hell, you know that?" She grinned.
"Yes, I know it. But you like it, don't you?" she stroked his lips with her fingers. "Don't you like it, Harry?"

"I'm crazy about it. I could kiss you forever. You were born to be kissed."

"Do you think I'm beautiful, Harry?"

"Yes."

"Let me hear you say it. Tell me how beautiful I am, Harry. Tell me."

"You're the most gorgeous woman I've ever seen or ever hope to see."

"And ravishing?"

"I could eat you up. I'm dying to eat you up."

"Do you like my legs? Do you think I have pretty legs, Harry?"

"My blood pounds every time I think about them."

Cora shoved her knee from under the cover and stroked her thigh. "Yes, I think they're pretty myself." The leg was almost against Harry's face. He fell upon it, covering it with hot, wet kisses.

Claude went right on snoring along. He was dreaming. Almost every time he went to sleep he had dreams. Some of them pleasant, some of them nightmarish. This dream started out to be a pleasant one. He was dreaming of days gone by, days when he was a young man in the Navy. Norfolk was a wide–open town then. Main Street was a sailor's paradise. There were taverns every ten feet along Main Street, and all the women a guy wanted, and there was the Gaiety, Norfolk's only burlesque house, and they had the hottest shows in the country.

The Gaiety was always packed with sailors. On Saturday nights there were so many sailors trying to get in to see the show that some of them had to be turned away. This almost always caused a ruckus and the manager was forced to call the Shore Patrol to quiet things down.

A Navy man's weekend would go something like this: He and a couple of buddies would have a weekend liberty. They'd hit Main Street first thing, get half–loaded on beer and booze, and then take in the show at the Gaiety. The show, always a sizzling one, featuring some of the country's most talented strippers, never failed to leave the gobs ready and primed for a night with a good–looking babe.

They'd have a few more beers and take off to the cathouses which lined Main Street like the taverns did. The dames worked in the taverns and in the houses. If a guy was lucky he found him a good looking babe in one of the taverns and romanced her into spending the night with him in a private hotel room. This was a big accomplishment and one to be proud of.

"The rest of you guys can run to the whores," he'd brag, "and spend your dough that way if you want to. Me, no! I like to work up my own stuff. I don't get a bang out of having to pay for it. Takes all the kick out of it." It was something he could talk about for months to come, how he was man enough to get a babe on his own. The fact that it always cost him more dough this way, he never admitted, even to himself.

In those days the rest of the city of Norfolk was practically non–existent as far as sailors were concerned. Every time they ventured away from Main Street they seemed to end up in the brig. The other, respectable sections of the city, were, in a way, off–limits. Many sailors were embittered by this fact. But the truth of it was that most of the Navy men were away from home and when they hit the beach at Norfolk they were ready for a good hot time, and since this wasn't their home, they didn't care what they did or whose daughter they made because they'd be pulling out in a few weeks anyway so what difference did it make?

Realizing this, the city fathers allowed Main Street to keep the gobs entertained in order to keep them away from the decent parts of the city. And they kept Main Street well patrolled, but open to anything within reason, and they had the city doctors keep the prosties inspected and free of disease.

In Claude's dream he again was on Main Street a day after the Fleet came in. On that day practically every gob was on Main Street dying for a date with a good looking babe. They'd been at sea on maneuvers for months and they were primed and rank and ready to a man. Tens of thousands of them. Main Street was so crowded you could hardly walk. The Shore Patrol was undermanned and worked to death trying to keep some sort of order.

The cathouses could not start to take care of the business. Sailors waited there in lines blocks long. They fought over places in the lines, tried to buy places closer up front, and tried to bribe the different madams into slipping them in the back way. They said the girls were doing their best to take care of the business. The girls kept little tubs beside their beds and as soon as they were through with one man the girl would hop out of hed, squat in the tub with disinfectant, dry herself hurriedly with a towel, and hop back in the bed to be ready for the next customer. There were so many sailors that this went on for days and days and the madams and pimps and behind–the scenes men made fortunes in minutes.

Later, when the Fleet again pulled out, it was discovered that three whores were dead. They had been "dated" to death. One of them had been dead in her room for hours and nobody knew. Everyone figured she was just catching a nap between sailors. She might have had a heart attack or a stroke. Having THAT much sex is maybe not natural no matter how fun it sounds. One girl said she thought the poor woman died because she realized that life was never going to get any better, maybe this was her only escape.

These things Claude was remembering in his dream. They were fond memories. He was a young and handsome guy himself then. All that was before he got out of the Navy and met Cora and fell for her, and had to have himself sterilized before she'd marry him because she was so afraid of having children and before he'd become so sexless himself and so fat and such a liquor lush. Yep, those were the days all right!

And then in his dream, he was in the Gaiety watching the strippers. The house was packed with sailors. Here and there you'd see a civillian, and down on the front row which always cost a lot more money, you could see some of the "swells" find their wives or girl friends down there s lumm ing. And he'd thought that a man must have a lot of nerve to bring a decent woman or his wife into that mob of woman–crazy sail ors. No telling what might happen.

He was watching a really fanatic stripper now. He squinted to see her. He was sitting about halfway back and he couldn't quite see her features.

There was something that struck him as being faintly familiar about her. She was exceedingly beautiful, he could see that much, and he noticed that as she performed the place became quiet, there wasn't a whisper, and the entire audience was held spellbound by her beauty and something else. The something else was her nat ural sex appeal. It stood out like a light. It was in the air of the theatre like a strong paralizing shock wave.

This stripper had a way of removing each garment in such a way that you forgot to breathe. Slowly..... slowly ... you held your breath until you were about ready to burst to see just a little more of her body.... and she watched the audience as one man and smiled a cunning little smile of complete assurance that right that moment every man in the place would practically commit murder to get to her. You could see that she enjoyed this, and that was the reason she was such a sensation.

Claude wanted to get a closer look. He couldn't understand the fee ling that she was familiar to him. Finally he got up and moved further down front where he could see better. He kept staring over the lights, trying to figure out who this fascinating woman was.

That's when his dream became a nightmare. That girl up there taking off her clothes before all those sex–crazed men was Cora, his wife ..... he could hardly believe his eyes at first, but it was her, and he looked around at the gaping faces staring at her beauty, and a rage began to swell up in him, and suddenly he was running for the stage, and before he could get there somebody grabbed him and held him back, and while he looked he could see another sailor leap upon the stage and grab Cora and wrestle her giggling to the floor and Claude could see that she was enjoying the fact that the man was trying to get to her right there on the stage and then he could hear the whole housefull of sailors yelling for the guy to "Take it! Take it!" for they had all of a sudden wanted to witness the harsh ravishing of this beautiful creature, and each man imagined himself as the guy on the stage, and they shouted encouragement to him.

Claude watched the guy up there with Cora struggling in his arms and laughing as the guy tried desperately to kiss her body, her bare breasts, shoulders, arms, as she twisted each portion away from him, and now the entire audience was on its feet and yelling, screaming for the guy to go on, "Take her! Take her! Take her! Give her everything you've got!"

With a mighty heave, Claude pried away from the arms which were holding him. Enraged, he dashed for the stage and leaped upon it and threw himself on the guy like a maddened tiger, dragging him away from the laughing Cora and beating him in the face as hard as he could and trying to kill the man, and when the man was half–unconscious on the floor he was stomping him in the face and he could hear the man moaning.....moaning.....and he could also hear Cora gigglin.....giggling... and Claude was so enraged that he stomped the man harder and harder there on the floor.

His dream commenced to play out. Cora, lying beside him there in the bed, was giggling softly at Harry's frantic efforts to have more of her than she would permit. She was joyous in the knowledge that she had reduced Harry to a helpless, frustrated animal. Now his quiet moaning was almost a whine. She smiled, twitching with a kind of exstacy.

Harry's soft whimpering was the most exciting sound she had ever heard. Oh, it was wonderful to play with Harry! He was such a passionate man! And his lips were full and warm and everywhere they caressed her body she tingled under their longing, searching, demanding hunger.

Claude came awake with a start and sat upright in the bed, blinking his eyes. Harry dropped quickly below the surface of the bed out of sight. His heart beating wildly, he crawled on the thick carpet through the door, got to his feet and tiptoed back to the sofa. He felt weak and frightened and nervous and completely frustrated.

"What's the matter, Claude?" he heard Cora ask.

"Huh?" said Claude's voice. "Oh, just dreaming.

"Had a teribble dream, a regular nightmare."

"It's from all that whiskey you drink," scolded Cora. "If you don't watch out you're going to be having the d.t.'s."

"Cora—now that we're both awake, do you want me to try to do something?"

"No. I'm not in the mood."

"You never are when I am," he said.

"Shhhh. Harry's in the living room."

"Oh, yeah, I forgot. But it's the truth, Cora—" He was talking quieter now—"we haven't done any thing in a long time together."

"I don't mind. I never did like to do it anyway. You know that."

"Is it because I'm so damned fat? Is that the reason yow don't want to anymore, Cora? I know I'm big as a hog but I can't seem to help it."

"You're okay. Now go on back to sleep."

"I had the damndest dream. It was about you."

"Never mind. Go to sleep. I'm tired."

He went on talking in a low voice. "Well, I guess I'm not sorry you don't like to do it, hon. I've sort of quit wanting to do it, too. Only some times I feel like I'm neglecting you. You're so beautiful and there'd be a million men who'd want to make love to you, and yet you never get any. It doesn't seem right somehow. I feel awful when I get to thinking about that. Here you are so beautiful and warm and all and tied down to a fat slob of a husband who never makes love to you. It must make you miserable, sweetheart."

"Never mind. I don't care a thing about men. You know that. I'd be scared to death to be left alone with a man. I've always been afraid to do anything, remember? I guess that's why I don't enjoy it. I'm satisfied the way things are."

"I think I'd die if you fell for some other guy and left me, Cora. I don't think I could stand it."

"There's nothing to worry about. I'm completely satisfied with things the way they are."

"You 're sure?"

"I'm sure, Claude. Now will you please turn over and go hack to sleep? It's late and I'm tired. We'll never be able to get up in the morning."

"Wonder how Harry is."

"Oh, I imagine he's all right."

"Suppose his fever's gone down any?" Cora grinned to herself.

"I don't know. I sort of doubt it though. They say that a fever gets worse at night."

"That's true," Claude said and rolled over. "Well, I hope Harry's feeling okay in the morning. Swell guy, Harry."

"Yes he is. He thinks the world of you, too, Claude."

"Yeah. Great guy. A real great guy. Trustworthy. You can trust a guy like Harry. Wouldn't be afraid to trust Harry with anything I had. He's a two–way guy. He does his share on everything. Not greedy like a lot of guys I know. Not Harry, he's not greedy a bit. That's one of the things I like about him. Not greedy."

This struck Cora as highly amusing but she said nothing. So, she thought, Harry's not greedy unless you give him something to be greedy about. And she had what it took to make him greedy and she had discovered that, once she'd handed him the tiniest little morsel, this Mr. Harry Baker suddenly became the absolute lv greediest human being in the world. He was starved for everything you wouldn't let him have .

CHAPTER FOURTEEN

Cora took off her jacket and said, flinging it on a chair, "How about a cup of coffee, Maryann?"

"Sure," said Maryann, "come on in the kitchen. I've already got some on the stove. Gee, I'm glad you stopped by, Cora. I was beginning to think you'd for gotten you had a little sister."

Cora laughed. "You know I haven't," she scolded. Maryann poured two cups of coffee and the two girls sat at the kitchen table and lit cigarettes. "Well," Cora asked, "tell me what's new. Any proposals lately? Met any new men? What have you been doing with yourself?"

"Same old thing," frowned Mary Ann. "I go out plenty, have lots of dates, but proposals, no. And I'm twenty–three! What's wrong with me, Cora? Why don't men ask me to marry them?"

Cora smiled. "Because you're too easy, honey. I've told you that before. You can't let men have you just by snapping fingers and then expect them to marry you! The trouble with you is that you give in too easy. No man wants a wife like that."

"But I can't help it!" cried Maryann. "I'm just too passionate. When a man wants me, it usually goes double and I want him also. I want it maybe more than he does, and I can't control myself. That's just the way I am. I'm built that way!"

Cora laughed. "You kill me, talking that way. I don't see how you can just let any man have you. Ugh! It makes me sick just to think about it."

"Oh, I don't let just any man. Some men don't appeal to me at all."

Cora suddenly thought of Harry Baker. "I know a man you ought to know. The two of you would make a good pair. He's the hottest–blooded human I ever saw!" A snicker escaped Cora. "And right now he is mortal-ly burning up!"

Maryann's blue eyes brightened. "Who is he? Is he good–looking?"

"Downright handsome. But his name's a secret. I'm keeping this one for myself."

"But why? You've got yourself a man. You've got Claude."

"I'm having some fun with him," smiled Cora.

Maryann frowned. "You're playing with him," she accused. "I thought you'd get over teasing men like you do. It isn't right!"

"It's fun to me."

"I never have understood you, Cora. You've always been crazy like that. Teasing the life out of men and never giving them anything. What in Heaven's name do you do it for? It isn't natural."

Cora took a puff of the cigarette between her slim beautiful fingers. "Oh, I don't know why I do it. I've just always got a terrific bang out of it. I like to go to work on a man and watch him squirm. I like to hear him beg. I like to see his eyes change as he gets to wanting me more and more. maybe it isn't natural, but it gives me a thrilling sensation. I like to get him helpless with passion. So hot he doesn't know whether he's coming or going. Don't you like to do that, Maryann?"

"Heavens no! Only time I got a man that hot I'd be so passionate myself I'd probably rape him!" They both laughed.

"You've been that way every since we were kids, Cora. I can still remember that Smith boy who lived next door. You tortured that poor boy out of his mind!"

"Yes, I remember. I had a lot of fun playing with him. I had him begging like a dog just to kiss my hand. He sure was funny. I'd work him up and then cut him off and he'd cry like a baby!"

"You ought to be ashamed of yourself, Cora. You know, I think you really hate men."

"I do not!"

"Yes you do! You hate men whether you realize it or not. If you didn't, you wouldn't like to make them suffer."

"I never heard of such a thing," snapped Cora.

Maryann sipped her coffee. "Let's change the subject. Tell me more about that man you mentioned."

"Nothing much to tell."

"Yes, there is. You don't kid me, Cora. He's something special, I bet. Come on, what's his name?"

Cora was smiling again. "Wouldn't you like to know?" she chided. "Oh, I might let you have him when I get through with him. He's a friend of Claude's."

"I bet you've got him in the same shape you had that Smith kid."

"Well, he's smoldering, I'll say that. If I let you two get together you'd be like a couple of eels!"

Just the thought excited Maryann. "Let me have him, Cora, let me have him! I know you've got him red–hot. Let me have him now! I want him that way!"

Cora laughed. "Not 'til I'm through with him."

"How long will that be?"

"I don't know. He's a lot of fun."

"And to think you only want to play with him!"

Cora·grinned. "That's right. Just play."

"Better not let Claude catch you."

"Don't worry! That's what makes it so good. This man is Claude's best friend. Claude trusts him implicitly. We even had him over to spend the night last night."

"Cora! You mean you're working on one of Claude's friends! How could you?"

"Oh, I don't know. Just makes it more interesting, I guess."

Maryann shook her head. "I'll never get to understand you if I live a hundred years. Cora, you're impossible!"

Maryann was amusing to Cora. Cora had always thought her younger sister to be slightly on the dumb side. She didn't know how to handle men at all, never had. Maryann just didn't seem to know how to say no to any guy on the make. Cora wondered how many times Maryann had thought she was in love with some jerk and thought the jerk was going to marry her. It happen ed all the time. It was a miracle she hadn't got herself in a mess before now.

Cora glanced around the little apartment. She bet Maryann had a man up here with her almost every night. Oh, well, let her have her fun! It was a nice little apartment, though. Maryann had a pretty good job, too. She'd been working at a switchboard in the hospital for about six years now. She made enough to take care of herself and keep well–dressed. It looked to Cora that some dope really would want to marry Maryann. After all, she was a very beautiful girl. Nice figure. Blond. Big blue eyes. And even though she was too passionate for any one man to keep her happy, it still seemed that some guy would want to marry her just the same. It would just mean that he would have to overlook a few things. Maybe she would outgrow her passion in a few years. Her bringing in money from her job ought to offset some of her faults. Oh, well, men were crazy that way. They want to have every woman they see, but they're only interested in marrying the ones they can't touch. Crazy world!

Cora picked up her coat. "I better be going. I'll come back to see you again real soon, Maryann. In the meantime, remember what I told you. If you want a man for a husband, don't give in to him. Be hard to get. That's the only way you'll ever get him interested in matrimony."

"I'll try." But Maryann was still excited about the new man Cora had been telling her about, and she was dying to find out who he was. She knew what Cora could do to a man, and nothing suited Maryann better than finding one that her sister had gotten all steamed up. It had happened before. A man that Cora had teased along if you could get to him soon enough, would pracically eat you alive and then give you the hottest loving you ever had in your life. The thought made Maryann twitch all over.

"I sure wish you'd tell me who Claude's friend is," she complained. "You're mean if you don't."·

Cora laughed. "So you're still thinking about that! You're crazy, Maryann. But maybe I'll tell you before long. When I'm through with him I'll hand him to you hot and sizzling on a silver platter. How's that?"

Maryann was pouting."Well, make it real soon," she pleaded.

As soon as Cora departed, Maryann ran to the telephone and called Claude.
"Claude,". she said, "Cora was telling me about a friend of yours who I should meet." She tried to keep excitement out of her voice. "The fellow who was with you last night. Do you think I'd like him, Claude?"

"Sure!" Claude boomed. "You and Harry would hit it off swell. Wonder why I haven't thought of it before."

"What's his last name, Claude? Cora told me but I've forgotten."

"Baker. Harry Baker."

"What does he do?"

"Car Salesman, Hell of a good guy. You'd like him a lot, Maryann. All the girls do.!'

"Automobile salesman you say?"

"Yeah, and a good one. Works for Brownley's Used Cars. You know, down on Granby."

"Oh, yes, I know where that is. Would you get us together sometime, Claude?"

"Sure thing . But why the rush? You got plenty guys chasing you,"

"Oh, I don't know. It' just a feeling I've got. The way Cora described him I think I'd find him real interesting, that's all. It'• just an instinct, you know us women and our instinct, Claude!"

Claude laughed "I sure do. You don't need brains. You girls don't need brains at all. All you. need is your instinct!"

"Quit joking. No, I mean it, Claude. I've got a peculiar feeling about this Harry."
"Okay, sugar, I'll fix it up as soon as possible. In fact, I'll call him right now."

"Oh, swell, Claude! You're a dear. Let me know, will you?"

"Just as soon as I talk to him."

"I'll be waiting." Maryann waited thirty minutes. Finally Claude called her back. "Can't reach him now, Maryann. Brownley's said he was home sick, he wasn't feeling well last night As a matter of fact he had a fever then. I tried his apartment but no one answered. Tell you what, though, I'll try again later. Then I'll let you know."

Maryann was disappointed. "All right, Claude. And thanks."

Maryann stripped and took a shower. Now, in her bedroom, she stood nude before her full–length mirror and surveyed herself. Her body was beautifully supple. Her breasts were firm and pointed. She glided her hands caressingly over them and down the voluptuous curves of her hips and brought her hands together be tween the thighs of her perfectly molded legs. A look of anguish filled the blue depths of her eyes, and her lovely face displayed an emotion akin to pain. With all of her beauty, she thought, she forever hungered for love. Why, she asked herself for the millionth time, why did she have to be constantly in need?

Men were such dogs! Such cruel selfish dogs! They satisfied them-selves and left her to suffer. That's what they all did. Every last one of them. Didn't any of them realize that a woman needs to be satisfied, too? Like Ray last night. He'd loved her twice, taking about five minutes each time. Then he was finished, and proud of himself at that. And she was only start ing. Ray was finished and she craved more. Lots more.

More and more and more! But all the men she knew were the same way. They were all selfish dogs! Maryann fondled her own body there in front of the mirror, and then she fell across the bed and wept dismally. Afterwards, she got dressed and went out and caught a bus to downtown Norfolk. She alighted at Monticello and City Hall. From there she walked through the Ar cade to Main and turned left. She put on dark sun glasses and continued. Finally, she arrived at a small hotel near the burlesque house. She went inside. The desk clerk recognized her and smiled. He was a thin, pale man with horn–rimmed glasses.

"Ah Miiss Snead," he said. "'Miiss Maryann Snead. How are you to-day?"

"Okay." She had always used the name Snead to hide her true identity.

"Room?"

"Yes. Can I have the same one as last time?"

"The one with bath? I think so. Let me see." He examined the register. "Yep, it's open." He looked up and eyed her hungrily. "Same deal?"

"Yes."

He handed her a key. "I'll be up soon's I can. Now, don't trick me, I want to be first! Get it? First! I don't want to follow anybody, hear? Then the sailors can have you, but not until I'm through. No tricks now!"

Maryann smiled. "No tricks," she promised. "Many other girls working?"

"A couple." He grimaced. "But no competition for you, Beautiful! They're beasts! Strictly worn–out old bags!"

"Then maybe I'll be rushed;" she said.

"You will. Plenty of sailors around. They'll be swarming in after the burlesque show is over. They got a hot stripper this week. The gobs come out with their tongues hanging down to their knees crying for a dame. You'll be busy all right not 'til after I'm through. I'll be up soon's I get somebody to watch the desk."

Maryann went up to her room and undressed. She always felt a little embarrassed to begin with, but she forgot the embarrassment as time passed into a sort of sexual oblivion. She was hardly undressed when the clerk came in. His name was Herb. He took one look, loosened his belt, and started to remove his tie and shirt, but the naked beauty of Maryann's lovely body was too much to wait for, and, seeing his anxiety, Maryann lay back on the bed with her feet still touching the floor and she closed her eyes just as his face sank into the flat of her belly.

Maryann sighed and readied herself for the sensuous joys to come. The pale Herb wasn't much to look at, but the way he started she always found pleasant. More men should do what Herb was doing now, she thought. A woman needs that to get her off in the right frame of mind. Finally, she lay soft and panting and Herb swung her graceful legs on the bed. The bed springs squeaked for a few minutes and then Herb was finished. But Maryann was now consunmed by passion.

''Don't leave,''' she pleaded. "Please don't!"

"I've got to," Herb said. "But don't worry, I've got a sailor waiting downstairs. I'll send him right up. Won't be but a minute."

"Hurry!". she begged. "Hurry!"

The sailors came one after the other, all through the night. She accepted them as one man, tried to convince herself that they were only one man, her lover, returning to her again and again, the supreme man, who a dared to love her all night, never tiring, never stopping. In this way, Maryann tricked herself into a sort of fantasy of satisfaction, a wonderfully enjoyable delusion.

CHAPTER FIFTEEN

It was hot in the small apartment. Harry looked at the little fan beside his bed. He cursed it. He could hardly feel any breeze at all. Might as well not even have the thing for all the good it was doing him. He wished he had more windows in the place. It would be better if he could get a breeze. He hadn't been able to get any sleep at all. That Cora Staley had burnt her image on his mind. He could not wipe it out.

He lit a cigarette and lay there smoking and sweating and staring at the white ceiling, remembering the events of last night. His long body stretched the entire length of the bed. He was in shorts. His clothes hung over a chair where he'd flung them. What he needed was a cup of coffee. He'd given up trying to sleep. He swung his feet to the floor and went to the kitchen and set aome coffee on. Then he went to the bathroom and brushed his teeth. He glanced at his lean, angular face in the mirror. A tough stubble of beard was beginning to show. Ought to shower and shave, he thought. Don't feel like it right now, though. Later, maybe. After he'd had his coffee.

He didn't think he'd go to work today. Wasn't up to it. In the mood he was in he couldn't sell a car if someone tried to take it away from him. He threw some cold water on his face and neck. It felt good. He dried and combed his dark hair. He felt some better, not much, but some. His dark eyes were slightly bloodshot and stung a little. He guessed he'd live.

At the apartment door, he got the morning paper and took it into the kitchen. The coffee was perking. He poured a cup. He sat at the table sipping the scalding coffee and glancing over the headlines. He lit another cigarette. Cigarettes and coffee were the best things for the way he felt. Just after nine he telephoned Brownley's and told them he wouldn't be in. He told them he was sick. Had a fever. Might as well stick to the line Cora had given him. For the first time he noticed that he was lonesome. He guessed it was natural. Most guys his age were married. They had a wife and one or two kids. He'd have to get around to that someday.

'He hadn't met anyone yet he'd marry, though. That was one thing he was going to have to be awful careful about. She'd have to be passionate, that was sure. No cold fish for him. And not only passionate, she'd have to be like him—wanting it to last for long periods at a time. Most of the hot babes he'd known liked their loving, but they got all they wanted in too much of a hurry to suit him. They wanted to stop too soon. They always left him not quite satisfied— even the best of them left him that way.

Maybe he was oversexed. Plenty of girls had told him he was. So what? So what if he was? There was nothing he could do about it, was there? Somewhere there must be an oversexed girl. That's what he really needed. When he found such a girl, if he ever did, they'd make sweet music together. He'd marry a girl like that provided he was making enough money to take care of her. That was another thing. He was going to have to concentrate more on his future, and where he was headed. He didn't want to remain a car salesman for the rest of his life, did he? When a guy reaches thirty three he ought to have at least some vague idea of what he wanted out of life.

Well, he'd like to own a used car lot of his own someday. He liked the car business. Plenty of money in it for the guy who owned the business. If he had a good location and had a few good, experienced sales men he could make a pile if he was on the ball. It was also one of the safest businesses a guy could be in. You hardly ever heard of a used car dealer going bankrupt. Well, cars were something everybody wanted. Men, women, and children. A man had told him once: "Stay in the automobile business. Hell, folks will go without food in order to buy a car!"

Harry had found this to be true. He grinned and shook his head as he remembered one instance. A sailor came on the lot one day and paid five hundred dollars down on a car. He kept the car for thirty days. Then he phoned Brownley's and told them he was leaving the car on Granby Street near 21st. "The key is over the sun visor," he said. "You can have her back now. My ship is pulling out and I gotta go. But man I've sure had me one big ball!"

Five hundred dollars to drive a car for thirty days! What a lark! Harry went back and plopped on the bed and stared at the ceiling some more. Nothing much else to do. He fell to thinking about his old ship back during his Navy days. Boy, that seemed a long time ago. He'd been a lot of places on that old tub. Practically all over the world. He'd seen a lot of things and done a lot of things. She was a cruiser, and he got to thinking back to the days when the war was at its hottest. They were somewhere in the Med, not far from Gibraltar. Some thing always going on around there. The German subs made that one of their favorite stomping grounds. They got many an American ship there, too.

He remembered the bodies floating all over the place. He remembered the little red lights bobbing on the water at night. Life–jacket lights telling them there were men out there, floating around, waving the lights for help. He remembered how careful they had to be in trying to rescue them because the subs lurked around the survivors waiting for a cruiser or any ship to attempt the rescue, They would throw a fish in your side if you even slowed down in those days. It was ticklish business.

He remembered laying in his bunk smoking and listening to the depth charges going off all the time out there in the dark water, and he remembered telling himself if he ever got out of this mess alive he was going to get out of this man's Navy soon as his hitch was up, and he wasn't going to worry about another thing as long as he lived. It took something like the war to teach a man that life was too short and uncer tain to worry about anything. No, sir, he was going to spend the rest of his life having a good time and trying to make some real dough. You had to have the dough in order to have the time.

He remembered Algiers and he thought about Marie. He met her at the bar in the Hotel Internationale. He'd just walked in and sat at the bar and ordered a drink, and she walked in and he thought, "Damn, she's good looking !" and she smiled at him as she passed him by, and he swung around impulsively and caught her arm and asked her if she didn't want a drink.

"Yes, I weel 'ave one weeth you," she said, and perched on the stool beside him.

"My name's Harry," he told her.

"Harree? Is nice!"

"What's your name?" "Marie."

"Glad to know you, Marie!"

They had a drink and some more girls came into the bar and Marie took him to the table where the girls were sitting. One of them was her sister, she said. "Can you buy us all a dreenk, Harree?" she asked. A lone ten–spot was all he had. He took out his wallet and opened it and showed her the ten.

"This is all. Fini, when gone," he told her. Marie reached into his wallet and took the ten. "For me, for Marie," she said. Harry didn't know whether to take the money away from her or not. Then he thought, oh what the hell! What if she does take me for the ten? Good–looking as she is, it'd be worth it. He shrugged his shoulders. "You got me;' he said. "Keep it. But you'll have to buy the rest of the drinks out of that. I'm busted. Flat! Fini!"

Marie smiled and patted his hand. "Harree is nice boy. No worree you. Marie not steal your monnee ! Marie take you weeth her."

"Where?"

"Moviee," she said. "We weel all go to the cinema. Okay?"

"Sure," Harry grinned. "Okay." All the girls were French. They left the bar after Marie paid for the drinks walked uptown and went to the cinema. It was an American film with the dialog changed to French. Harry couldn't enjoy it very much. The place was crowded and hot. He held hands with Marie as they watched the movie and she squealed and went into spasms of emotion over every small incident. The French were certainly excitable, Harry thought. They sure were full of life.

He was glad when the show was finally over and they were out in the fresh air again. Then all the girls left except Marie's sister, and the three of them walked a long way up a hill to the sister's apartment. The apartment was on the second floor and contained several large windows overlooking the city and the harbor. It was much cooler up there. A gentle breeze flowed through the room. It was mid–afternoon.

The girls took off their dresses down to bras and, panties, just as though it was the natural thing to do. Harry said to himself, hell, and stripped down to his shorts. Marie's sister disappeared into another room and Marie and Harry stretched out on the bed by the window where the cool breeze would blow over them.

"Is time for siesta," she said.

"No," said Harry, "is time for love."

Marie laughed. They were lying facing each other. She put her pink–tipped fingers on his lips.
"Haree is nice," she said. "Harree like Marie?"

"Crazy about you."

''Nice lips, Harree has," she said, running her fingers over them. "You kiss girl, Harree?"

"Sure I kiss girl. Come here," he said. He kissed her.

"No. No. No. No! I no mean like that. I mean you kiss girl." She nodded downward.

"No, hell,.no!" Harry said. "I don't kiss girl like that. That's just for the French guys!"

"No. No. No. No. Nol American guys too. They kiss girl. French boys and American boys no difference."

118

"Like hell!" Harry said.

"Marie knows. American boys ashamed. French boys no ashamed. Marie know plenty American boys. All kiss girl same as French boys."

"Not me," said Harry. "No this American boy!"

Marie smiled through her dark eyes. Her raven black hair lay askew over the white sheet, and she stretched like a cat and her body was a thing of voluptuous beauty. "Harree no tell truth," she said, her fingers on his lips again. "Harree has nice full lips. Boys weeth full lips always kiss girl."

"Hell, is that the only way you French want it?"

"No. No. No. No. No! Marie want to make love with Harree. Harree no have to kiss Marie! No. No. No. No. No!"

"Well, let's get with it then!" She made him wait a minute. She slid off the bed and went into the room where her sister was. Harry couldn't see through the door from where he lay. A minute later the sister came into the room wearing only panties. Harry had to catch his breath. He had never seen such beautiful breasts on a woman in his life. They pointed firmly straight out. She ignored him completely and went to a bureau and fussed around in a drawer.

Harry started to get up, then hesitated. He managed to tear his eyes away from her. He had suddenly realized this was some kind of a test. She came to the bed and asked him for a cigarette. He gave her one and she bent over him and he lighted the cigarette for her. He did not once let her think he was affected by her beauty. She thanked him and returned to her room. Marie came back to him almost instantly. She seemed happily excited about something. She crawled up on the bed beside him and commenced covering his face and lips with passionate kisses.

"Hey, what goes?" he said.

"Harree is nice hoy. Marie like Harree veree much." Harry knew now how wise he'd been in not making a pass at Anna, the sister. He'd passed the test with flying colors! Yes, he was in like Flynn! The kissing continued, getting hotter and hotter all the time. Harry was beginning to realize he had hold of a live, flaming volcano. She had a way of biting him. She'd bite his lips, his neck, the upper part of his arms, and his shoulders. Sometimes she bit him so hard he didn't think he was going to be able to stand it. Amazingly he found that the pain carried a sort of pleasure with it. He tried biting her a few times around the neck and he could tell that it plainly added to her excitement.

He slid off her bra and her breasts were identical to Anna's, if not more so. These French gals sure had beautiful knockers! Immediately he started biting them, one after the other. He'd bite until she whimpered and then he'd ease up a little. This seemed to drive Marie completely out of her mind. There was a knock at the door. Angrily, Marie went to answer it. She spoke in French to someone in the hall. She closed the door and called Anna. Anna came and opened a crack in the door and talked in whispers to the person outside. Harry could hear enough to tell it was a man.

Finally, after much bickering, Anna let the door open. An elderly man about sixty–five came in. He had a concerned expression on his flushed face. Inside, he glanced at Harry and Marie, nodded, grabbed up Anna's hand, and slobbering over it, followed her into the other bedroom.

"What's that old codger up to?" Harry wanted to know.

Marie looked at the closed bedroom door with disgust.

"He comes to see Anna. He gives Anna much moa– nee,"

"For love?"

"Yes, he loves Anna,"

"Hell, I'd think he was too old to do anything! These French guys must never give out!"

"He kisses Anna," Marie said. "Nothing else, Too old. He very old man. Not too old to kiss. He kisses Anna and gives her much monnee,"
Christ! thought Harry. "Does Anna like it?"

"But certainlee! Is good to be kissed. Girls like it veree much! American girls no like to be kissed?"

"How the hell would I know!"

She put her finger on his lips again "Such nice mouth," she said. "Poor Harree no kiss girl. Marie feel sorree for all American girls if all American boys like Harree and no kiss girls!"

"Let's forget it," said Harry. "Maybe I won't do it for you, but I can sure as hell raise Cain with it otherwise !" He jerked off her panties and his shorts and flung them on the floor. He pulled her to him, her smooth firm body tight against his own, Their hips went together and her arms locked tightly around the back of his head, her lips were crushed harshly to his and she opened the sweetness of her mouth to him catching her breath in little gasps. When he opened his eyes her white skin seemed even more beautiful, and the raven black hair lying against the sheet more lustrous, and the white arm around his head and against his cheek smoother and more glorious than anything he had ever seen, and it was so beautiful that he was forced to turn from her mouth and suck the beauty of her arm.

This went on and on and on. Every few minutes Marie would stiffen and tremble and then, suddenly, like something gone wild, she would bite him until he almost screamed from the pain, and then she would relax and they would settle down to a slow rhythmic touching of hips and bellies. On and on and on. Once she whispered, "Harree is very much love. Harree no stop Muhreeeee."

"You can say that again!" Harry echoed. If there was one thing he liked it was a long, drawn out session. No quickies for him. He always felt like he could go on forever. Finally, Marie was ready to stop. "Me fatigue," she said. "Hurree, Harree."

He thought the room was being turned upside down because his brain whirled with the ecstasy of it, and then he was screaming....

Afterward, his mouth was dry. Marie got up and brought him a glass of wine. He lay there with the cool breeze playing over him sipping the wine and smoking. He thought about the old man in the next room. He tried to form a mental picture of what the old man was doing with Anna right then. He strained his ears to see if he could hear anything. He couldn't. After a while, he did hear the bed springs raising particular hell. He looked at Marie and nodded toward the door.

"That old fellow is giving it hell," he said.

Marie frowned. "Is no old man," she said. "Is only Anna. Old man is kissing Anna now."

"Damn!" said Harry. "Somebody oughta toss that old codger out on his tail!"

"No. No. No. No. No! Anna be veree angree if you try to stop old man now!"

121

"She likes it, huh?"

"She like eet veree much. Hear bed springs? That is Anna. Yes, she like it veree much!"

Harry continued to listen while all sorts of mental pictures flashed through his mind. Then he was wanting some more of Marie. "No," she said. "We weel go to my apartment. Then there will be more love, oui?"

Harry was disappointed. He didn't want to wait. His body was crying again. "Why waste time?" he said. "Then when we get to your place we can really get down to business. I think you like it as much as I do."

"Yes! But it is late. We must go. There weel be more love for you. Oui! Much much more love. You Weel see, yes. You come weeth Marie."

He could tell that her mind was made up. They got dressed. He nodded toward the bedroom door. "Going to say anything to Anna?" She shook her dark head, smiling.

"No, Anna weel know. She does not like to be disturbed when the old man eeze weeth her. She weel keep him a long time, oui!"

It was a long walk to where Marie lived. Algiers was a hilly place. To get anywhere, you went up one hill and down another. It was a metropolis. French, Moroccans, Spanish, Italians, Arabs, and a few Americans. No one seemed in a hurry. Marie's apartment was not nearly as nice as Anna's, and he soon knew why. Marie had responsibilities. She had a kid, a boy of four years.

"My husband was keeled fighting the Nazis," she said. "He was officer in the French Army. He never saw his son."

"I'm sorry," Harry said. "You must have had it tough."

"Oui! Veree bad!"

"How do you live? How do you manage to take care of yourself and the boy?"

Marie appeared embarrassed. "I make monnee from the American boys," she said. "It eeze the only way. My babee," she nodded at the little boy, "he would starve if I deed not." Harry acted as though the news came as no consequence.

"Well, a person has to live," he said. "I think you deserve a lot of credit. Actually, you are helping the boys as well as yourself."

"You do not mind, Harree? I like you veree much, Harree. Oui!"

"Of course I don't mind."

She had a tiny bedroom and a tiny kitchen. She went out and returned with a small portion of ice and a bottle of wine. She fixed a stew and the three of them ate and drank wine. Harry played with the boy. He was a likable little tyke. But the ravages of war were in his bright little face. Harry felt a twinge of pity. This boy had probably already lived a lifetime. No doubt he'd gone to bed hungry many many nights. He'd hidden under the shelter of Marie's arms as the hideous Nazi planes dropped the bombs in the streets and on the buildings. She fixed the boy a place to sleep in the kitchen. Harry kept the wine and a glass beside the bed on a small table.

Someone knocked on the door. "Don't speak," Marie whispered.

"Who is it?"

"Some American boy mebbe."

"Come to make love?"

"Oui. He weel go away."

They heard footsteps departing.

"I'm costing you money," Harry said.

"Marie no care. Marie like Harree. Love only Harree tonight. Oui!"

"I'm grateful," he said.

He turned to her, pulled the voluptuous body to him, and a moment later he was again ecstatically happy, knowing that now, for the first time, here was a woman who could give him all he wanted. So she was a whore. So what the hell did that matter? Within two hours she was yelling for him to stop. He didn't want to stop, couldn't think of stopping. Marie grew angry and burst into a sudden, violent fit of temper.

"Peeg!" she screamed. "Peeg! Peegl Peeg! Get out, peeg! Go out'. Go back to your ship!"

Hurt and sober, Harry dressed and she pushed him out the door and slammed and locked it.

"Marie no want your monnee !" she screamed. It was then he noticed that his ten dollar bill was lying crumpled in his hand.

CHAPTER SIXTEEN

Harry snapped back to reality. The things that happened during the war were a long time ago. Many other things had happened. He thought of them from time to time. They were things he would never forget. But where was it all leading him? He found himself wondering more and more where his life was going, where he was going to end up. A man should have at least some idea of what he wanted. A man couldn't seek to satisfy his passions forever. His promise to himself, made back during the war, to never again worry or care about anything, now seemed an empty promise.

What he really needed, he guessed, was a woman. A good woman. Something to give him stability and responsibility. He'd thought of this too, from time to time. But what kind of woman? He'd known just about every kind of woman there was. He had never met the woman he'd want to spend all his days with. In fact, he didn't believe he could be true to any one woman. He didn't believe a woman lived who could give him all the love he wanted. Oh, he supposed there was, all right, but he'd never been even close to finding her.

Cora might be the one. He didn't know. But she was Claude's wife. She had what it took to set a guy at white heat. He'd never wanted a woman so bad in his life as she'd had him wanting her last night. She had an instinct for firing the imagination, making a guy want her so bad he could simply die. He had to have Cora. Just once. Just once any how. He had to know how it would be to love her completely. Thoroughly and completely. Since last night he'd suffered terribly from a sense of unfulfillment. He had a feeling that this longing would last forever, until he had her. Once. At least just once.

Right now, just thinking of her, his blood was reaching the boiling point. Curiously, just thinking about her irritated him. What a dame—and what a gruesome night! The more he thought about her, the angrier he became. What a case history she'd make for Freud! Kinsey could've written a chapter on her alone! That is if he could figure her out. Oh, well, it takes all kinds, Harry thought.

The shrill ringing of the phone jarred his nerves. Let it ring. Probably someone from Brownley's. The phone continued to ring, this time with a stubborn insistence. He picked up the receiver and swallowed hard. It was Cora.

"Harry," she cooed sweetly. "How are you?"

"How the hell do you think?" he asked gruffly. Suddenly he felt mean and sore as a boil, and before she could answer he let loose with a barrage of sarcasm. "When's the next performance?" he wanted to know. "Any new features, or are you keeping the same old act?"

He could hear her gasp. "Listen," he said evenly, and his voice sounded nasty, "lay off me, Irresistible! I've had it and I'm not buying any more." Then he hung up. He smiled grimly. That business was over! That should take care of that weird bitch! He sighed deeply. "Aw, the hell with her!" he muttered half–aloud. He flopped back on the bed.

Someone knocked on the door. Startled, Harry swung his long legs off the bed and went to answer it. It was Jean. "Hello, Harry. Heard you were sick."

"Jean! For crying out loud, what are you doing here?"

She smiled. "Move out of the way and let me come in and I'll tell you." She brushed past him.

Harry peeked out to see if anyone was m the hall to notice. "Nobody knows I'm here if that's what is worrying you," she said. "I made sure of that!"

"Where's Bill? I'd hate like hell for him to find out you were up here alone in my apartment. He'd shoot the living hell out of me!"

"You worry too much," she said. "Forget Dad. He hasn't the faintest idea where I am. That's the truth."

"How did you know I was supposed to be sick? And another thing, how did you know where I lived?"

"It's simple. Spady told me."

"I thought you said nobody knew you were here."

"Well, just Spady, that's all. He wouldn't tell."

"No, Spady wouldn't tell." Harry ran his hand nervously through his dark hair. "Well, now that you're here, what's on your mind?"

She smiled an impish smile. "You know what I told you. You're my man and if you are sick I'm going to look after you. Where's the broom? I'll start by giving the place a good cleaning. Then I'll fix you something to eat. I'm a pretty good cook if I do say so. Heck, a man can't wait on him

128

self. He needs a female to take care of him. And the female for you, is me."

"Thanks, Jean, I appreciate the thought. But I'm not sick. Not sick at all. Just tired. Had a had night that's all. So you needn't bother. You just run along now. I'll see you tomorrow, huh? It's not wise your being up here with me."

"Now Harry," she pouted. "don't be cruel. I've been crazy to see you ever since Dad interrupted us yesterday. Don't be mean to me, Harry."

Seventeen, thought Harry. Just seventeen. Look at her, just sweet seventeen. Damn he wished he had some guts. All that fresh young beauty just begging him to take her. Fresh lips moist as dew. Firm body just itching, itching with the vitality of a girl just turning woman, itching for sensations that are due the beautiful.

And she was so very beautiful.

And Cora had left him dying with passion. Suddenly remembered how passionate Jean got in the car yesterday. And nobody but Spady Mears knew she was here and Spady could be trusted.

"Jean, if you insist on staying, okay, but you know what's bound to happen, don't you?"

Her grey–green eyes avoided his. She twisted her back to him, flipped her long black hair up naughtily with both hands and said,

"I've a general idea."

"Make yourself at home. I'm going to the kitchen and take me a big slug of bourbon. I need it."

"Can I have one?"

"I'll bring back the bottle." He got the booze some glasses and a pitcher of ice water and took them in the living room, pulled a chair over to the sofa and set the stuff on it within easy reach. He also equipped the chair with an ashtray.

He could tell that Jean was trying too hard to look nonchalant. He knew one thing, she looked enticing as all hell. She was wearing a pink skirt, no stockings, and a sheer white blouse that displayed the points of her firmly molded breasts. She was enough to make a guy's eyeballs perspire. He sat on the sofa beside her and poured bourbon into the glasses. "Say when."

"Not too much for me," she said. "I don't like mine too strong."

Harry found himself wondering if she'd ever really done any drinking. Probably not to amount to anything. More than likely she was a little scared right now and only wanted the shot to bolster her courage. He wondered. "I bet you've never had a drink m your life," he said.

"I have too! I drink all the time."

"Stop lying. You don't. Look, take it easy. You don't have to impress me. This is Harry, remember?"

"All right, then," she frowned. "I'm lying. I've had a bottle of beer once in a while, but that's all. Seems like I can't fool you about anything!"

Harry smiled. "Then quit trying."

"Guess I might as well."

Harry lifted his glass. "Well, here's happy days. Chug–a–lug. Down the hatch and all that." He swallowed a big slug of the bourbon. Jean turned hers up too. She nearly gagged but she managed to get it down and catch her breath, but only with difficulty. Harry laughed at the expression on her face. "Yeah," he said, "I can see you're an old whiskey drinker all right. A regular old–time boozer."

"It took my breath!"

"You'll be all right. The next one will go down a whole lot easier."

"Gosh, I hope so!"

Harry put down his glass and lit a cigarette. "Well, Jean, now that we're all liquored up, what do you want to do next?"

"Stop teasing me, Harry. You're treating me like I was a kid again."

"Sorry. But I can't for the life of me see what you want to fool around with an old guy like I am when there are thousands of guys your own age who I know would give their right arm to romance a beautiful babe like you."

"We've been through all that," she scolded. "Anyway, the boys of my age always have to tell every thing they know. If they get a girl, they run around bragging about it to all their friends. Juveniles! That's what they are!"

"Yeah, that's true. I hadn't thought of that." Her face was a little flushed.

"Oh, I'm beginning to feel that drink! The warmest glow is spreading all over me. I feel wonderful!"

She stretched her slim white arms out luxuriously. Around one of them was a little golden trinket that enhanced the luster of her skin, She flexed her slim, perfectly groomed fingers like a cat flexing its claws, and then, suddenly, she grabbed him by the ears and threw herself across his lap and pulled his lips down to hers. Harry was taken by surprise. She might be inexperienced, he thought, but her natural urgings were certainly pleasant.

CHAPTERSEVENTEEN

Their lips lingered together for a long time. Harry felt his heart commence to pound, slowly at first, then faster and faster. He felt the liquor warming his blood too. Alcohol always made him more passionate, made red lips redder, white arms whiter, beauty more beautiful. He could feel the freshness of her youth, an exciting emotion fired in his brain. This was a new experience, even for him. The danger of her age made her ten times more tempting. He was throwing aside all reason, he knew, but now it was too late to turn back. He was a kind of fatalist that way. One started, it was to hell with the rest, let come what may! Anyhow, what red blooded man could resist such beauty as Jean's?

After their lips separated, Jean smiled warmly up at him. "Do you want me to take off my clothes?"

Harry felt a sense of disappointment. "Just like that?" he asked.

She appeared hurt. "Isn't that what you want me to do?"

"Well, yes, I suppose so. But look, honey, you're being too easy, don't you know that?"

"I admit I haven't had much experience," she said. "I was only trying to please you, Harry. I thought that would make you happy."

"Oh, it does, in a way It makes me very happy to know you want to please me. But listen, Jean, I'll tell a secret—no man likes for a woman to just lie down and say come on. Now I'm only telling you this for your own good."

"But what am I supposed to do?"

"Lead up to it," said Harry. "The secret is to make a man want you very badly before you give in. Make it interesting. Always leave some doubt in his mind about whether you'll let him have you or not. You have to work up his passion; drive him half crazy, if you can, and then, not before, let him have you. But always keep the doubt in his mind."

"I appreciate your telling me this," she said. "I know I have got a lot to learn."

"No man respects a girl who will give in at the snap of his fingers. That's just simple nature. A man loves the chase. If it's too easy, it's not much fun. Understand?"

"I'm beginning to, Harry." Her grey–green eyes brightened. "Harry! Would you teach me? Would you teach me how to drive men out of their minds! I'd love to he able to do that! I could practice on you, and you could tell me what to do and what not to do! Will you do it, Harry? Please!"

Harry laughed. She was certainly a little eager beaver. But she was attractive as hell even in her ignorance of love––making. "Sure," he said, "I'll try. It should prove interest ing. Real interesting."

She sat up and took his arm. "What's the first thing I should do? Oh, this is going to be fun!"

"Maybe," Harry grinned. Suddenly he felt a little foolish. "Well, I guess the first thing to tell you is a man's sensitive spots–places that arouse him."

"You mean like his lips?"

"Yes. But that's only one. His ears, cheeks, and along the hairline of his neck–they're places no woman should forget."

Jean was all excitement over this new venture. "What else?" she urged.

"Well, of course, about the most important thing is a man' s eyes."

"His eyes?"

"Sure. What he sees. In other words, you don't show all of yourself at once. You show just a tiny part, then a little more and a little more. For instance, if you pulled your skirt clear up right now I'd merely see a beautiful pair of legs, But if you inched it up a small bit at a time, the suspense and desire to see more would drive me nuts. Get what I mean?"

"I think so. I'm beginning to understand what you mean. What else?"

"I can't think of more, unless it's a man's you–know–what. Everytime you rub against his you–know–what you're really throwing coal on the fire."

'"That all? I want to get started! I'm all excited just thinking about it!"

"All right, we'll get started. Now, the purpose is to see just how passionate you can make me. I've told you how to do it, so le't's see if you can take care of the rest. Remember, you've got everything you need to work with, you're beautiful, you have a knock–out figure, your legs and breasts are perfect, and your hands are lovely. You've got everything. All you have to do is use what you've got, that's all."

"Ready?" she grinned.

"Ready. Let's see you go into action."

"Oh, goody!" Jean said excitedly. She sat up. He lay back. She put her hands on his cheeks with her fingertips touching his ears. She bent to-ward him and kissed him softly, just brushing his lips. Then she brushed his lips again with her own wide open. Her fingers toyed with his ears. She brushed across his lips again, this time lingering a moment, and it had suddenly become delicious to Harry and he attempted to hold her with his own. As soon as he did, she moved the rose petal softness of her own away from him. When his head twisted to follow, she separat-ed their mouths with the pink palm of her hand. A sudden sense of her sweetness enveloped Harry. He grabbed her and tried to capture her lips again, but she, smiling in an impish way, kept their lips separated by her lovely fingers.

Becoming thoroughly aroused faster than he had expected, Harry grabbed her wrist pulled her hand away and caught her open lips for just a maddening, fleeting second. Then she was twisting away and his mouth dove for the smooth curve of her neck and shoulder, and he found himself pulling the blouse down over the whiteness of her shoulder, and covering it with his trembling lips. She twisted away, and he caught up a bare arm and made a path of kisses down it to her hand, and he turned the hand palm upward and burrowed his flushed face in it.

At this point, he noticed the blouse had slipped up exposing her mid-rift. Almost too roughly, he pulled her lengthwise on the sofa and madly kissed the beautiful soft flesh of her firm tummy. Now almost beside him-self, he jerked the blouse over her head. She wore no bra and her firm, pink–tipped breasts pointed straight up at him and sent him into hysterics of desire. He fell on them hungrily, but she maneuvered each away from him just as he captured it, and she rolled away from him facing the back of the sofa, leaving the petrifying beauty of her back exposed to his. burning lips, and he smothered her with kisses, the curve of her upper arm, the gentle slope of her side down to her waist. Here he saw that her skirt only partly covered her thighs. What he could see of her creamy white legs and thighs drove him wild with excitement. He yanked at the skirt and plastered her legs with his lips.

"How'm I doing?" she asked.

135

Harry could hardly catch his breath long enough to speak. "Too good," he mumbled. "Too damned good!"

Jean laughed. "I thought I was doing pretty good myself, Harry, I've got you hot as a firecracker, haven't I?"

"You ain't lying! I'm worse'n that."

"You want me to slop?"

"Hell no! Hell, hell, no! The only thing is, I'm getting serious now. I want to get down to business!"

"Oh, no," laughed Jean. "That's not what you told me. I can't do that now. I don't think I want to at all."

"What are you talking about?" he asked his lips following the sweet line of her leg.

"Doubt," she said. "Remember? You said to create doubt. Harry, I don't think I'll let you love me all the way."

"Yeah, but I didn't mean for you to pull that on me! That part is for the other yokels!"

"Oh, no, it's for you too, Harry. I'm only following your own instructions."

Harry groaned to himself. What had he done? Worked himself into a trap? He wanted her now more than he'd ever wanted any other woman. She had his blood at the boiling point, there were no two ways about it. He'd told her how to do it, and now she'd turned the tables on him.

"I've got to have you!" he blurted.

"No, Harry, not this time." She lay there on the sofa, a beautiful young creature, bare from the waist up, her thighs bare, and Harry's lips rushing up and down her thighs. She smiled to herself as she watched Harry's head. Jean was a devilish girl actually. She feared nothing and was eager for life and every thrill life had to offer. Now she was thrilled with the passion she'd aroused in Harry. Watching him adore her, she was filled with a sense of power she had never before known. Some instinct told her that at this moment Harry was help less to resist her beauty.

A new idea filled her devilish grey–green eyes with delight. She wondered if she could make Harry want her so badly he'd kiss her. She'd

heard that was a thrill that was simply out of this world. She'd give anything for a thrill like that! She wondered if she had enough power over
Harry to make him go that far. After all, he was practically devouring her
legs; he was almost there now. She'd also heard that if you could make
a man kiss you you had him hooked for the rest of his life....and that's
what she wanted the most..,. to hook Harry in such a way he could never
break away from her. Maybe if she could just get him a little hotter...

She placed her hands on the back of his head. He was kneeling on the
floor. Softly she caressed the nape of his neck, his ears. She could hear
his breath coming in gasps. Suddenly, she sat up and lifted his head
pulling the pink skirt down almost to her knees.

"That's enough, Harry," she said, holding his mouth in her palm, letting
him see only the bare white inches of thigh above her knee.

"Oh, no," he groaned. "Don't stop me now!"

"But you said–"

"To hell with what I said! Don't stop me now!"

She felt the pull of his head downward as his lips again sought her legs,
and she let him drag his face down until she felt the flame of his lips on
her again, and she held her hand on the skirt and the other hand on his
head, and each time he moaned "please" she let his lips urge the skirt
a little higher up her thigh. He was going to! she thought excitedly. He's
going to kiss me! She knew it! He couldn't help himself. All she had to
do was make it seem difficult to him. Keep that gentle, resisting pressure
against him. Oh, he was coming higher and higher. Thrill after delicious
thrill swept over her lovely body. After more delicious moments of this,
she felt her body twitching in readiness, felt herself puckering for the
clash of his mouth. She was ready to swoon with anticipation.

The telephone was ringing. The sound of it got through to him slowly.
It was ringing and ringing and ringing. Jean tensed a little but ignored it.
Harry was trying to freeze the sound of the ringing out of his ears. His
brain was on fire; he'd burn out the grating sound. The telephone continued ringing and ringing and ringing. After each ring there was a little
pause, and at each pause he prayed fervently that was the last.

Ring. Ring. Ring ring ring.

"Goddammit!" he swore aloud. "That son of a bitch–that lousy son of a
bitch!"

He went to answer the damned thing. When he didn't want the phone to ring, the son of a bitch would ring its damned ass off. He felt like he could kill whoever it was. There was a murderous glow in his eyes. Jean still lay on the sofa. Her breasts were rising and falling sharply. Her grey–green eyes stared upward hazily.

"Hello!' Harry said.

He found himself listening to the hum of a dead line. The party on the other end had hung up. "Son of a bitch! Lousy son of a bitch!" He slammed the receiver down. Now he was wondering who it had been. They had certainly rung a long time, whoever it was. He ran a hand through his hair. It might have been Spady. Spady may have wanted to warn him that Hill Vincent or somebody was up to something. Maybe wanted to tell him Bill was on his way over here.

This thought made him a little nervous. He felt guilty as hell anyway. But he was going through with this come hell or high water. She'd been had before. She'd said so herself. One more time wasn't going to hurt anybody.

He went back to Jean. She had pulled the pink skirt down partially covering the delicious whiteness of her legs. Harry reached under the skirt and pulled her panties down over the firm curve of her hips and flung them to the floor.

"Let's get something done. I'm ready to explode."

Jean said nothing. He unbuttoned her skirt with trembling hands and pulled it away. He was becoming almost frantic. "Help me," he pleaded. "For God's sake help me!"

"Harry, please. I've heard it hurts the first time. Please be easy, Harry." His heart jolted. He stopped breathing. Then he rolled off onto the floor and doubled up and held himself.

"What's wrong, Harry?"

His voice was low, hardly above a pained whisper. "Get your clothes on and get out, Jean. Get out now! I mean it!"

"But why, Harry? Why?"

I've been every kind of a heel, Jean, but I've never started a girl off .... and I don't want to start you off. Hell, if you're a virgin."

"But I wanted you to be the first, Harry. I wanted a man to be the first, not one of those pimply–faced kids... I wanted you!"

Harry's body was crying out for her. He was actually in pain with desire. But where would it end? He knew how he was, once he got started. It'd be too late then. She'd be crying for him to stop in a short while. She'd be hurt and she'd despise him for not being able to stop hurting her.

"Please come on, Harry. Please. Don't leave me now."

"But you don't know how I am," he said. "Once I'm loving a girl I can't stop. I'd hurt you, you don't know how much."

She twisted on her side and was smiling at him. "I don't care, as long as you're the one doing it." Her hand was on his face. "Please, darling, please. It's not as if I didn't love you. I do love you, Harry. You're the only man I've ever loved. All those things I told you before were just part of an act, something to make you notice me."

"You're kidding," Harry mumbled, amazed.

"No," she said. "No one has even touched me but you. I couldn't bear having anybody else's hands on me. Only you, Harry. You're the only man I'll ever want."

The sudden simplicity of her admission, combined with her clean youthful beauty there before his eyes, was too much for any man to resist. This put a new light on things. Love. He hadn't thought of that. Then, how did he know it hurt a virgin? He'd never had one, had he? So how the hell could he know so much about it? Perhaps the feeling he had for Jean was love also. He'd never felt exactly like this with other girls. There was something different here, something new and wonderful and terribly thrilling. Maybe this was it.

He got back on the sofa beside her. Jean turned her wonderful body toward his. She lifted her head and opened her mouth to his. She helped him and it was like entering the kingdom of heaven. Her little cries filled him with a sense of tenderness he'd never known, and her mouth had the exquisite taste of dew–laden flowers, and the grey–green of her eyes was a beauty that consumed his soul. Something so strange was happening that he lifted his head and stared. He saw it then in her eyes, her softly smiling eyes. Her beautiful eyes were saying, "Hello, dear, recognize me?"

Still, he didn't speak., Where was that insatiable lust that had so long been with him? Why didn't he desire further ravishing of her body, as he had other women? He was relaxed and at ease, except that the whole affair with Jean had so far opened into a mystery.

"What is it, Harry?" she asked softly. "Was I all wrong for you?"

"No. I'rn not quite sure of anything right now. It c ould be that. "

"What, Harry? she was eager to know.

"Maybe it's something you have for me that other women don't have. Somehow I feel different from what I've usually felt after I've… "

"After you've had a woman, Harry?"

"Yes, putting it bluntly, after I've had a woman."

"I've always wanted to be something else to you besides just another woman. I've wanted to capture you… capture your heart… even prove to you that I'm something besides a love–hungry young girl who doesn't know what she wants."

He avoided her eyes. Perhaps he knew then that she'd accomplished her mission; that she'd proven her point, without ever having argued it. But should he tell her? Did he dare? Was it real, or was it only his imagi- nation that she'd been the first woman who satisfied him?

"Harry, don't think I'm stupid enough not to know that you've had scads of women and that I'd certainly have plenty of competition. But I've fig- ured it out. Some of the women in your life weren't really in love with you. They couldn't give you what I can, because of the difference in how I feel toward you."

Harry wasn't at all pleased that she had to tell him something about himself that he should've known; though if what she'd said was true, what more did he need?

"Look at me, Harry," she said, smiling when he gazed into her eyes. "I felt you! my whole body was pulling dissatisfaction from you. It was almost an unguent, drawing pain from a burn. You feel something deeper than sex for me, Harry!"

"I hate to say it, Jean, but I think you're right. Somehow, I've never real- ly thought I'd find this–you, as you are, and the effect you've had on me. I'm going to make a bid for you, Jean!"

"You don't have to bid for me, Harry. I'm yours. Just take me, give me a chance to prove myself."

"Your dad, Jean. Remember what he told me? And I think he meant it."

"No. Maybe at first he did. But after he was through ranting and raving, and he'd cooled down, he realized that I had to make my own decision about the one I love and want to marry. He knows I'm here. I told him that the next time he saw us together, we'd have decided what we intended to do."

"Have you decided, Jean?"

"Yes. I've decided."

"Then, so have I."

"Are we together, Harry?"

"That's my decision. Yours?"

"God, Harry, yes! Wouldn't you know?"

His lips sought hers and they clung together, almost desperately. Instantly she became a citadel for him, against the world of women who'd never satisfied him and the insatiate lust he'd known for them.

ADDITIONAL NOTES

The note below was pubslihed in the the edition of the book which came out around the time of the indictments and is being offered here for the sake of completion and context.

GOVERNMENT ATTACKS FABIAN BOOKS

Fabian Books are under attack. It is charged that our boo\cs are unfit for public reading because they deal with sex too intimately. We believe that the government attack is ill considered and insulting to you, our readers. We do not believe that you must have your reading material spoon fed to you by government officials to decide for free citizens what they should or should not read. We attempt to publish honest, true-to-life stories depicting life as it is and not necessarily as it should be. Our books treat with sex of course since sex is an important aspect of life. The attack upon us stems from prudes who would, in the Victorian manner, confine discussions to the impeccably regular kind which a reverend mother could contemplate with equanimity.

BUT MOST THINK ING PEOPLE AGREE THAT THIS OSTRICH-LIKE APPROACH TO SEX IS QUITE WRONG AND HAS CAUSED GREAT HARM TO THE MENTAL HEALTH OF VAST NUMBERS OF PERSONS!

Whether our books are good or bad literature is not the point, of cqurse. The best test of their worth is the market place: if they fill some need, if they give some pleasure, they wil l be purchased and read and not otherwise. Since your freedom to read what you choose is also at stake we would apprecite your writing and advising us in as GREAT DE-TAIL AS POSSIBLE what you think of the Fabian books you have read. We are particularly anxious to know if, in your opinion any of our books deal too intimately with sex. Finally, let us know whether you believe the books should be suppressed or should be allowed to circulate and be distributed TO ADULTS.

OUR OTHER BOOKS

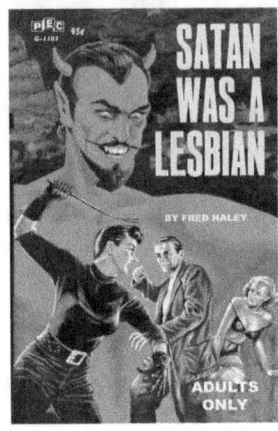

SATAN WAS A LESBIAN

The book that launched a thousand t-shirts is another novel from the pulp era whose title seems to inspire sales without really reflecting the story within. Very cool cover art in our newly restored format. Available at Amazon, eBay and on our own website.

ISBN 978-159362-318-0
$12.95

A PICTURE PERFECT AFFAIR

From our sister company The Hotwife Club Press comes a modern bit of erotica. A Picture Perfect Affair tells the story of a boudoir photography session gone sideways and the start of a new lifestyle. This is a novelette that include AI generated images for your enjoyment. Also available as an e Book.

ISBN 9781593623203
$9.95

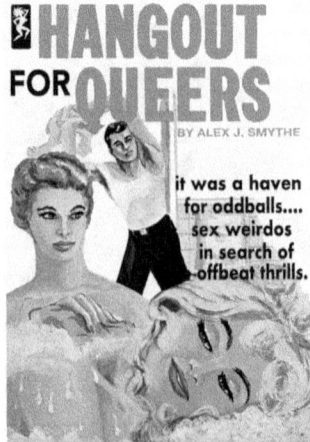

HANGOUT FOR QUEERS

Not what you would expect from the book title, there are no actual queers or looks at queer life in the book. Instead this is a pretty standard sleeze book with our standard of restored cover art and AI generated illustrations.

ISBN 978-1-59362-324-1
$12.95